I0691646

Kaleidoscope

Kaleidoscope

Susan Bohnet

WALNUT SPRINGS PRESS

This is a work of fiction. The characters, names, incidents, and dialogue are products of the author's imagination and are not to be construed as real, and any resemblance to real people and events is not intentional.

Text copyright © 2019 by Susan Bohnet
Cover design copyright © 2019 by Walnut Springs Press
Interior design copyright © 2019 by Walnut Springs Press

All rights reserved. This book, or parts thereof, may not be transmitted, stored in a database, or reproduced in any form without prior written permission from the publisher, except in the case of brief quotations embodied in critical reviews and certain other noncommercial uses permitted by copyright law.

Printed in the United States of America.

ISBN: 978-1-59992-174-7

Acknowledgments

I am thankful for my family and friends for their continued support, and grateful for all the readers who wanted more of Mo's story. A huge thanks also goes to Walnut Springs Press for believing in these books, and my editor Linda Prince for her keen eye and enthusiasm.

1

Birthday Hints

Mo got into the passenger seat of the car and closed the door. "What's this?"

Sitting in the driver's seat, Joe Parker held out a purple gift bag with yellow and purple tissue paper spilling over the top. His face was red, and the hue seemed to be intensifying by the second. "It's a birthday present."

The cars on either side of them backed out of the parking spaces, crunching snow under their tires. Over the high school football field, clouds skittered through the sky as though they had other places to be. Joe shifted and fidgeted, holding the gift on his lap like an offering about to be placed on an altar.

Mo turned in the front seat and met his eyes. "Today's not my birthday, Joe."

"Oh, I know. I didn't forget your birthday . . . it's in three days. Sometime in the early morning hours, like two or three AM."

Mo grinned. "It was actually closer to five," she said.

"I was close," said Joe, triumphantly.

"Five PM." She smirked and accepted the proffered gift. "Can I open it now?"

Joe nodded. "Happy birthday, Mo."

The blue of the sky behind his head seemed to swim around his smiling face. It was like the blue background so often used in school pictures. Mo paused long enough to bring the image firmly into her memory. Then she flung the tissue paper out of the bag. It fluttered through the confined space, turning their world purple and yellow for an instant.

She was turning sixteen! Maybe he would finally ask her out on a date. She peered into the bag. There was a large, white plastic bottle and an old-fashioned alarm clock, the kind you had to wind up. "What?" she whispered. She raised her eyebrows and pulled out the bottle—Pantene shampoo. Joe smiled. Mo set it on her lap and reached into the bag a second time to retrieve the alarm clock. "Okay . . . uh, thanks, Joe."

"You're welcome." He gave Mo a wide smile, and one of his eyebrows was arched higher than the other.

"Is this a hint or something?" she said.

His blue eyes flashed. "Uh-huh."

"Oh." Her heart sank. She washed her hair almost every morning. If she played basketball, she washed it right after. Her hair was clean—maybe a little wild the next morning after being slept on, but pulled back in a ponytail it wasn't so bad. At least, that's what she'd thought.

Disappointment washed over her like a wave. *Keep it together, Mo.* "Well, thanks, Joe. Only a true friend would tell it like it is."

She opened the car door and had one foot out before he laid his hand on her arm.

"Wait," he said. "I thought I was going to give you a ride home."

"Thanks, but I think I'll walk. It's not that cold and my boots are warm."

Mo climbed out of the car. Joe was still talking, but she swiftly closed the door and hurried away. She wasn't going to make it home before the tears came, so she changed her course and strode into the school. With the purple gift bag in one hand

and her backpack hanging from the other, she hurried through the almost-deserted hall to the nearest girls' restroom.

She'd had such high hopes for this birthday, but Joe hadn't asked her out after all. If there was one thing she understood it was that things could change. Your house could burn down one winter night, and your father could die from smoke inhalation just when you thought he was starting to get better. Next to those things, a birthday date was nothing.

Mo looked in the mirror above the sink. "Just once more," she whispered to herself and turned to lean against the sink as she let her mind go back to that day in June.

There was a banging noise, and the van came to a halt across the highway from the park with the sausage monument. Mo and Joe and a bunch of other teenagers spilled out of the sliding doors to look at the smoke coming from the hood of the van. Then she and Joe were side by side on the grass while they waited for help to arrive. The sunshine was warm on her face as they talked—as they connected—and then Joe had playfully chased her. When he caught up to her, he smiled timidly, grasped her hand, and said he would ask her out on her sixteenth birthday.

Now here it was, November 9, three days before the big birthday, and his gift to Mo was a "hint" that she needed to spend more time on her appearance.

Since that day in the park, Joe's smiles had seemed warmer, his teasing more comfortable, like a private joke. He never mentioned dating again, but Mo figured it was understood. Obviously not. All the admiration she thought she saw in his eyes was just friendship, plain and simple. Asking her out was the furthest thing from his mind. He probably didn't even remember what he'd said.

Mo went into a bathroom stall and pulled out a length of toilet paper. She blew her nose and wiped her eyes as she emerged from the stall. Not wanting to walk home carrying the gift bag, she transferred the shampoo and alarm clock into her backpack.

"Toughen up, Matheson," she told herself. She and Joe would spend time together in the coming weeks. She would rein in her emotions and it would be fine. He was one of her best friends, and maybe it was safest to keep it that way.

She glanced in the mirror and shouldered her backpack. Her eyes were red, but she was prepared to face the world. She pulled open the door. There was Joe, pacing in front of the restroom. The world she could face, but Joe? Not so easily. She fought the desire to flee as he came to her and stopped. He didn't seem to know what to do with his hands.

"What?" he said. Then his eyes riveted on hers. "I'm sorry. What did I do?"

Oh, great, he can tell I've been crying.

When Mo didn't answer, he said, "Please let me drive you home."

"Okay."

The Acadia was now the only car in the student parking lot. Mo got in and took a deep breath while she waited for Joe to get in his side of the car. He started the ignition and pulled onto the road. "Can I buy you a hot chocolate?" he asked.

"Okay."

Mo's eyes wandered over his profile as he drove. No other guy even came close to Joe—no one was as nice, no one as good-looking. His dark-brown hair was cut short over his ears, and a little longer on top. It suited him, and he was just plain cute. *Friendship is better than nothing,* she reminded herself.

Joe pulled up to the A&W drive-thru speaker and ordered two hot chocolates. Then he inched the car around the curve and up behind the car already at the pickup window. "It's so narrow," he said. "I didn't realize that when someone else was driving."

Mo managed a smile. "You've only had your license for two weeks."

Joe grinned. Then the grin faded and he looked at her. Twice he seemed ready to speak but turned to glance out his window instead. The silence was terrible.

Finally, the car ahead of them received three bags through the take-out window and moved on. Joe pulled up, paid for the drinks, and handed one to Mo. "Lagasse Park?"

"Okay," Mo replied.

A few minutes later, Joe parked at one end of the park. He and Mo headed toward the wooden walkway at the edge of the lake. The snow had been cleared from the path, and it was warm enough out that they didn't need gloves. The sun shone over the icy surface of the lake, creating a beautiful winter scene of grooves and ridges.

"I'm sorry," Mo said finally. "I guess I don't take criticism very well." She and Joe walked a few more steps. "And maybe it was just a joke, but if it wasn't, that's okay."

"A joke?" He sounded offended.

"Okay, so it wasn't a joke. Um, that's okay."

"Why would I joke about something like that? I know we're friends and if you want to just keep things that way . . . but no, I wasn't joking."

"Then tell me honestly. What about my hair needs help?"

Joe's forehead wrinkled. "Your hair is beautiful."

"But—"

"But nothing."

"But you think I should wash it more often?" Mo said, pretending she was talking about a far less personal topic. Her tone would have been the same if she had asked, "Do you think the town should clean the streets more often?" or "Do you think the school hallways are wide enough?"

Joe motioned toward one of the benches that overlooked the lake. Reluctantly, Mo sat. She didn't want to look him in the eye. The bench was cold through her jeans.

"I am such an idiot," Joe began, "for thinking you would know what I meant." He reached out and touched Mo's hair. "You really thought I was telling you that you need to wash your hair more often?"

"Well, yeah." She bit her lip. "That's not what you were saying?"

"No. Not at all." He crossed his arms and looked out over the lake. "I guess it was kind of a joke."

"Oh sure, now you're just trying to get out of trouble."

"Thanks for smiling." Joe held her gaze for a moment, and the past years of friendship seemed to flow between them and fortify him. "I guess I've thought about the day in Mundare too many times over the past months. You probably don't remember, but I asked you if I could ask you out when you turned sixteen."

"I remember."

"Do you remember what you said?" When Mo didn't immediately answer, Joe continued, "You said you'd go out with me as long as you didn't have to wash your hair or something."

"And you want me to be washing my hair?"

"I also gave you an alarm clock. It was supposed to be a reminder to not sleep in so you'll be free to go out with me Thursday night. Here's the alarm clock so you don't oversleep, here's the shampoo in case you run out."

"Oh."

"I'm sorry, Mo. Just because I remember that day so well doesn't mean you do."

"It was in June, but—"

"I know. It was a long time ago. And if you don't want to, just say so. We can still be friends, right?"

"Actually, I was just thinking the same thing."

"You were? So you don't want to go out?"

An excited little butterfly seemed to be fluttering through Mo's chest. She smiled coyly. "You haven't asked me yet."

Joe smiled back. "Would you like to go to a movie with me on Thursday night?"

Mo paused to let the feeling enter every cell in her body. "I'd love to."

On their way back to the car, Joe began to laugh. "What?" Mo said, touching his arm.

"I can't believe I didn't realize how rude it would look to give you shampoo."

"At least there wasn't any deodorant in that bag."

Joe laughed. "Or a toothbrush."

"Or mouthwash."

"Or those Odor-Eater things for your shoes."

"Or zit cream."

"See, I could have messed up a whole lot more than I actually did."

2

An Exception to the Rule?

Nathan couldn't think of Maury as Mo. She was his little sister. So was Bailey, of course, but Maury was even younger. He clenched his teeth as Bailey and Maury spoke. All he could think was *No way,* over and over. With each repetition of those two words, he got more and more frantic. Maury was too young and too trusting.

"What do you mean you have a date?" Nathan said finally. "You're not even sixteen yet. And you are supposed to only date in groups."

Maury rolled her eyes at him. "We're not going out until Thursday, Nathan. I will be sixteen by then."

Her birthday. *Sixteen? Really?*

Bailey set aside the book on her lap and sat a little higher in the pale-green recliner. She glanced up as if about to say something, but then glanced down again. *Come on—help me out here,* Nathan thought. She should back him up, maybe talk about the dangers of steady single dating. But Bailey just gave him a sad look and didn't say anything.

"Why do you have to date him, anyway?" Nathan asked Maury. She glared at him like he had asked why it was necessary to breathe. "You're friends. That should be enough when you're minutes away from sixteen. Dating isn't mandatory at sixteen, you know."

"I know," she said, stretching out the words.

What would Dad say if he were still here, still alive? A weight settled on Nathan's chest, and his breath came in shallow little bursts. There would always be the empty hole in their family. None of them could fill it.

He paced the living room. Their new house was on the same lot as the one that had burned down, but this one looked completely different. He turned toward the living room window. The orientation was the same but the view was lower, and all the bedrooms were on the main floor. Nobody said it out loud, but at least with this house, it would be easier to escape in case of a fire.

Nathan went into the kitchen, opened the refrigerator, and stared inside without seeing. *Maury and Joe Parker?* She really was old enough to date—or would be in a few days. And little Joe had actually asked her out. But he wasn't so little anymore. Nathan and Joe had both played basketball after the youth activity last week at the branch meetinghouse, and Joe was almost as tall as Nathan. And he wanted to date Nathan's sister.

"Didn't I tell you a long time ago not to get all chummy with Joe?" he called in Maury's direction.

She walked into the kitchen with her hands on her hips. "Do you have a reason to dislike Joe, or is the fact that we are going out on Thursday the only thing you have against him?"

Nathan grabbed a bag of pepperoni sticks out of the meat keeper and slammed the fridge door. "He's . . . " Nathan took out a pepperoni and bit off the end. "He's going to take you to a movie?" He growled in the back of his throat. "You don't need to be sitting there in the dark with some guy."

Bailey huffed as she rounded the corner to join them in the kitchen. "Maury shouldn't have to pay for my mistakes," she said. "I know you're just worried about her, Nathan. I think you are great for caring, but Maury isn't me, and Joe, sure as heck, isn't Wade."

"This doesn't have anything to do with you and Wade."

"Of course it does." Bailey slid onto one of the stools that fit under the island in the middle of the kitchen. "Maury's not me," she repeated. "You don't have to treat her like she can't be trusted."

"It's not about trust," Nathan said after several seconds of silence. "It's about a choice or two that can get out of hand. We always think we're strong enough to handle things, but we're kidding ourselves, especially if we think the rules apply to everyone but us."

"And you just don't want her to make the same mistakes I made," Bailey finished.

"When we start dating, we're supposed to date casually, in groups," Nathan said. "That's the counsel from our prophets." It was the part about dating that everyone seemed to forget.

"But this is Joe," Maury said. "I know I can trust him. Nathan, you know what the Parkers are like."

"So you think you're an exception?"

Maury lifted her chin. "Maybe I am." She turned on her heel and strode out of the kitchen and into the hall leading to the bedrooms.

Nathan turned to Bailey. "When did she get an attitude?" Maybe he *was* being extra cautious because Bailey had gotten pregnant when she was fifteen and unmarried. Still, everyone should be extra cautious. And he was sure Mom would agree with him one hundred percent.

3

A Trip to the Zoo

Walking down the hallway at school the next morning, Mo was acutely aware of the sounds of locker doors banging shut and students chattering. "Did you see that TV show last night?" "I didn't finish my homework." "What time's the game on Friday?" "Where's my math book?"

Mo dropped her backpack in front of her locker and started to turn the dial on her lock. "Hey, Mo!" called Jessie Crowchild. "How'd it go yesterday?" Jessie, whose glossy black hair just reached her shoulders, shoved her basketball into her locker and snapped the lock closed.

"Hi," Mo said.

Jessie leaned against the locker next to Mo's. "Does this mean Joe didn't ask you out yesterday after all?"

"Uh, well . . . " Mo took a breath and released it slowly. "Actually, he did ask me out. We're going to see a show Thursday."

"Right on your birthday, huh?" Jessie smirked. "He couldn't even wait for the weekend."

"Did I hear right?" It was Hannah, squeezing in between Mo and Jessie.

"Yeah. They're going to a movie," Jessie reported.

"I told you he didn't forget," Hannah said. "And he still wanted to ask you out. Why didn't you call me last night?" She bumped her elbow into Mo's arm. "You and Joe!"

All day, Mo's emotions swung from excitement to something else—something more like anger or regret.

After lunch, Jessie, Hannah, and Mo went to the gym and practiced ball-handling drills and foul shots. When their coach arrived to teach his third-period class, Mo jogged over to him and said, "I won't be at practice today. I have to drive to Edmonton with my sister."

"Shopping?" He rolled his eyes a little.

"No, Coach. Something important. I wouldn't miss practice if I didn't have to."

He nodded. "Yeah. I know that about you."

"I'll work extra hard at practice tomorrow."

"Sounds good. Have a safe drive."

Mo and Bailey left school soon after lunch. "I need to stop by the house," Bailey said as she drove toward home.

A few minutes later, Mo was clomping into the house and kicking off her boots, with Bailey right behind her. Mo was bothered about missing practice, but even more so, she was bugged about Joe. She had been waiting, hoping, wishing for this date for so long. Now that the time was actually here and he had asked her out—however awkwardly it started—was she supposed to turn him down? She imagined the humiliating conversation starting out with "My brother doesn't trust you and me in a darkened movie theatre unchaperoned."

Nathan was ruining everything. Mo had floated into the house yesterday and immediately told Bailey all about the date lined up for her sixteenth birthday, but Nathan had promptly ended her happiness. *Nathan and his overprotective attitude!*

"I'm almost ready," Bailey said. She stuffed her wallet into her purse and went into the kitchen.

Mo grabbed a photo album from the shelf in the living room.

It was her only album, and it contained only recent pictures since every other picture was lost in the fire. She sat cross-legged on the couch and flipped to the last page of the book. There was a picture of Joe and his friend Darius. Mo had snapped this shot at the last school dance. Both guys wore jeans and long-sleeved dress shirts. The guys were grinning, and Darius had laughed and said, "We're basically twins. If Joe looked a little more Asian, you couldn't tell us apart." Besides the different ethnicities, Darius was at least two inches shorter. In the picture, Joe's right arm was extended toward the camera as though he was asking Mo to dance, which he did right after she lowered the camera. So many times she had she looked at this picture and imagined the invitation wasn't for a single dance but for a date.

She flipped the pages and looked at her photos in order. Pictures of the house being built, pictures of the first day of school, pictures of her, Hannah, and Jessie. She and Hannah had been friends forever, and now Mo suddenly had two best friends. She paused and then turned the page. There was a picture of Mo with Bailey—and the baby. Mo flipped the album closed and returned it to the shelf. *I'm going out with Joe on Thursday night. They aren't going to stop me. Dad would've said, "Have a great time on your date, Maur." Or maybe "Be home early, you two."*

"Hey, Dad, I have a date with Joe," Mo whispered.

Bailey came into the room, her gaze darting around as though she was looking for something.

"Are you okay?" Mo asked.

"I don't know. I can't think of better adoptive parents than these guys. They send pictures and letters, and now they invited me to the Edmonton zoo with them. Thanks for coming with me. I really don't want to drive there alone."

"The weekend would have been better, of course, but . . . "

"Their coupon is only good Monday to Thursday."

"Or summer?"

Bailey shrugged. "I hear the tigers are a lot more active now. The roads should be good. Mom called and said they were fine this morning."

"We're meeting Mom at her office first?"

"Yeah, and she'll come with us. It just feels so weird, Maury. I haven't seen the Andersons and . . . Brooke since the day in the hospital. It all happened so fast."

"The adoption people said that was best."

"That's what they said, but I'd just been through seventeen hours of labor and delivery, which was harder than I ever imagined, and then I held the baby for only a few minutes, and then I slept, and suddenly the Andersons were there to take Brooke away."

Mo nodded. It was going to be weird for her, too. She didn't know these people and didn't really want to get to know them. Brooke would be four months old now. Bailey had shown her the pictures the Andersons had sent. Brooke had thick blond hair like Bailey's, but with more natural curl. In one of the pictures, she was lying on the floor lifting her head up and reaching for a rattle—she almost had it in her hand and looked so proud of herself.

Bailey read and reread the letters Laura Anderson wrote to her. She probably had them memorized.

Bailey gave Mo a look. "Are the Andersons really as wonderful as they seem, Maury? Is Brooke really happy?"

"Now's your chance to see first-hand."

Bailey picked up a lip gloss from the coffee table and put it in her pocket. Her movements seemed disjointed, erratic. "I'm terrified," she whispered before turning away. She flung open the hall closet door and pulled her coat off a hanger.

"I'll be right back," said Mo. She strode down the hall, knocked on Nathan's bedroom door, and opened it a crack. Nathan was lying on the bed. "We're going now," Mo told him.

"When does Jordy get home?"

"At 3:45."

Nathan waved Mo into the room. He pulled off his earphones and sat at the side of his bed with his feet flat on the floor. "Good luck today."

"Thanks. Bailey's really nervous."

Nathan nodded slowly. "I'm sure it will be good for her . . ."

"I'm not so sure. She's stressed out. And she gave the baby up. Why go see her now?"

"At least Mom will be there."

"We need to get going." Bailey's voice echoed a bit in the hallway. She peeked her head into Nathan's room. "Ready?"

"I'll get my other coat, for the zoo," Mo said.

Heading down the hall, she heard Nathan's voice. "I . . . I didn't mean to hurt your feelings before . . . about Maury and her date."

Mo said nothing.

"I know. Don't worry about it, Nathan," Bailey replied. "You didn't say anything wrong. You're right, she should date in groups."

Traitor, thought Mo.

"Thanks for letting me take your car," Bailey told Nathan.

"I know it was hard to give Brooke up, but you made the right decision, Bailey."

"I know. Brooke is much better off with the Andersons. They seem like good people and they love her." Bailey paused. "But I love her too." Her next words were so soft Mo almost missed them. "And I loved her first."

"You were willing to give her a better life. She'll understand that someday."

"Thanks, Nathan. I needed to hear that right now." Bailey cleared her throat. "I better go."

During the two-hour drive to Edmonton, Mo had to keep pointing out that Bailey was driving at least ten kilometers over the speed limit. The roads were pretty clear for the middle of winter so it wasn't dangerous, but if she got a ticket, both Mom and Nathan would freak.

They passed a farmhouse with a wide porch running along at least two sides of the house. A girl who looked about five years old sat swinging in the porch swing. She wore a snowsuit, boots, and mittens. Mo laughed. "She must really like to swing."

"It seems like a peaceful life," Bailey said. "You work the earth—you plant and you harvest. Your kids play around on porch swings, and you have a dog and a few cats." She clutched the steering wheel. "There was that one couple I could have chosen, the one who had a farm on the east side of Edmonton. They had chickens and farmed something. Brooke would have had room to roam, and she would have learned to work hard and take care of animals." Bailey shook her head. "I can't keep thinking of all the choices. They were probably all good people, and any one of the couples would have been good parents."

"You didn't just pick the Andersons' name out of a hat," Mo pointed out. "You thought about it a lot before you chose them."

"I know. I just wish I could forget about all the others."

Silence settled in the car, and then Mo said, "I heard you agree with Nathan before we left."

Bailey glanced over at her, then back at the road. "So?"

"So, you're supposed to stick up for me."

"Would it be so terrible to go on a double date?"

"No. But why do I have to?"

Bailey shrugged. "You don't *have* to. It's your choice. And Joe is really a cool guy. He's just cool in all the important ways."

"And he's incredibly cute," said Mo.

"That's true, too. Not what I was referring to, but true."

They chuckled.

Eventually, they turned into the parking lot at their mom's city office. Bailey killed the ignition and took a deep breath. Mo checked the time. They were twenty minutes ahead of schedule.

Mo and Bailey walked across the parking lot while the sun shone, valiantly trying to warm the winter day. The advertising agency where their mother worked was on the second floor.

She mostly worked from home, but several days a month she came to the city.

Bailey paced the office while Mom flit about talking to people and putting things away on her desk. Bailey plopped into the chair next to Mo and said, "My stomach is churning. Maybe this wasn't such a good idea."

"You don't have to go," Mo said.

Bailey jumped up and paced. A couple of minutes later, Mom pulled on her coat and they left the office.

"Calm down, Bailey. The zoo is close to here," Mom said. "We'll be on time."

They got in her car, Bailey in front, and Mo in the backseat. Bailey huffed and placed her purse on the floor between her legs. Mom turned to her. "Are you all right, Bailey?"

"I'm scared, Mom." Bailey sounded about five years old.

"We could cancel," Mom said gently. "We have the Andersons' cell-phone number. We wouldn't have to give a reason. We could just say it's not going to work out for today and maybe another time."

"I've been looking forward to seeing Brooke," Bailey said.

Mom nodded. "The amount of contact you have with them is up to you. And all the letters and pictures are quite a lot of contact."

"I know. But I do want to see her."

"We could leave right after the picnic if you don't want to stay for the zoo."

"Okay. But I'm not sure if I can eat anything."

"I'm sure the Andersons will understand."

As they drove, every picture Mo had seen of Brooke flashed through her mind like a slide show. The child was still a young baby but seemed to have her own personality already. Four months old. It didn't seem that long ago.

They pulled into the parking lot of Storybook Zoo. "It's rather chilly for a trip to the zoo," said Mom. "And to come in the middle of the week! But I suppose using the coupon was important to the Andersons." There was a note of condescension in her voice.

Bailey frowned. "You think they should have paid the extra money and come on the weekend."

"It would have been better for us," Mom said.

They parked and got out of the car. Bailey linked arms with Mo as they approached the entrance. "Things were so much simpler when we were little," she mused.

Mom tightened the belt of her faux-leather jacket. It was a warm day by winter-in-central-Alberta standards. Bailey released Mo's arm and adjusted her teal-blue scarf. Mo slipped her stretchy gloves out of her pocket and put them on.

"I'm surprised the zoo is even open at this late date," Mom said.

Date. Mo's thoughts jumped to her date with Joe. When she told Mom that he asked her out for her birthday, she had said, "Sweet sixteen and your first date." Nothing about dating in groups.

Mom paid for three tickets and they entered the gate to the zoo. "Where are we supposed to meet?" There was an edge to Mom's voice.

"At the train," Bailey said. "There they are."

Bailey fell a step behind Mo as they walked toward the couple. The man was tall and slim with especially angular features. His face seemed all corners. The woman was several inches shorter than her husband. She had wavy blond hair that was shorter than the last time Mo saw her.

Mo hung back with Bailey, who looked pale and was shaking her head slightly. "Her hair's different," said Mo.

"It's like she's a different person entirely—some stranger who made off with my child."

Mo sometimes dreamed they were back at the hospital and she was coaching Bailey through her breathing exercises, and everything that happened afterward. It was still fresh in Mo's memory.

Bailey's gaze shifted to the stroller. The baby was bundled up in a thick pink coat that made her arms stand out from her sides. She had grown so much in four months. She had weighed seven pounds three ounces at birth and hadn't been able to hold her head up or control her hands or focus her eyes. Now she leaned forward in the stroller, clutching the padded bar in front of her. Curls poked out of the pink hood, framing her face with golden wisps.

Laura Anderson called, "Here you are!" She hurried to Bailey and wrapped her arms around her like an old friend. Then Laura stepped back and said, "We're so glad you're here."

"Thank you for inviting me," Bailey said mechanically. Her gaze kept returning to the stroller.

"Well, do you want to eat first or take the train tour?" Tom asked. The man's eyes were soft and his smile warm, in contrast to his rigid features.

"The train?" Bailey said. It was a question not an answer, but Laura and Tom got in line. Mo, Bailey, and Mom followed. On the train, they sat behind the little family.

Laura and Tom took turns holding Brooke and pointing out animals. The train returned to the station, and they all walked to the picnic area among the trees. Laura brought out cold chicken sandwiches and potato salad from a cooler. *You don't really need a cooler in this weather,* Mo thought.

"Thank you, this is a very nice sandwich," said Mom.

Mo echoed, "Yeah, it's great—thank you." She thought of commenting on the monkeys or the zebras they saw from the train, but the animals weren't really important. The zoo was just a backdrop. They were there to see Brooke.

When they finished eating, Laura lifted Brooke out of the stroller and handed her to Bailey. "Why don't you take her to see that little group of ponies in the petting zoo." Laura pointed to three tan, docile creatures with two other children around them, and a darker pony walking away from an older boy.

Group—in groups. Apparently, Nathan's words were going to haunt Mo every moment.

Brooke didn't seem especially interested in the animals, but her gaze rested on Bailey, Bailey smiled. Just four months ago, this little child had been curled up inside Bailey's belly.

Mo looked at Mom to say something to that effect, but Mom's eyebrows were low and the scowl on her face kept Mo silent. Mo joined Bailey and they walked to the petting zoo.

"Pony," said Bailey when they reached the fence.

"Eee," said Brooke.

The horse must've been used to such noises, because its left ear twitched and that was it.

"Nice pony," said Mo.

Brooke gurgled and said, "Eee."

"She's so cute," Mo said.

Bailey grinned. "She's absolutely adorable."

Bailey carried the baby to three of the ponies, then a sheep and a goat. There were ducks waddling among the larger animals. Mo lost track of time. Eventually, Mom caught Mo's eye and motioned for them to return.

When Brooke saw Laura's outstretched arms, she squirmed away from Bailey and almost dove at her adopted mother. "Did you say bye-bye to the horsey?" Laura said.

"And say hi to Mommy," Tom said.

Laura was Brooke's mother. Bailey was just the "birth mother." Mo looked at Bailey. *She's probably thinking that too.*

They walked from one animal cage to the next, and Bailey shook her head when Laura asked if she wanted to push the stroller. Tom tried to point out a red panda, but Brooke was more interested in a paper cup that was blowing end over end down the walkway. Tom placed a tender hand on his wife's shoulder when he spoke to her. They were a happy family, Mo decided, and Bailey had helped that happen.

It was growing dark already, and with a glance at Brooke's red nose and cheeks, Laura declared they should probably get going. Chatting with Mo's mother, Tom guided the stroller toward the exit.

Laura dropped back with Mo and Bailey. "I think I've thanked you a hundred times for choosing us, but I'm going to do it again," Laura said, wrapping both her hands around Bailey's arm. "I'm so glad you wanted to come with us today. I wanted you to see what a wonderful little girl she is and how happy you have made us. We take her to church every Sunday. The only week she missed was when she had an ear infection."

"An infection?" Bailey exclaimed.

"The doctor said ear infections are quite common." Laura chuckled a bit. "It was amazing how quickly she got better when we started antibiotics."

"Oh."

"I'm trying to be a good mother, Bailey. I don't want you to worry about Brooke. And money won't always be as tight as it is now. Tom's new business is in the early stages, but I'm sure things will pick up."

Bailey nodded. "You seem like a wonderful mother."

4

A Change of Heart

It was the day before Mo's birthday. She should have felt great—after all, she had a date with Joe Parker the next night—but she woke up cranky.

As she walked to school, Nathan's words tumbled around in her head. *"Do you think you're the exception?" "What about the counsel to date casually, in groups?"* There was no getting away from it.

The bell rang. Hannah had Language Arts first period, and Jessie and Mo had math. "See you guys at lunch," Hannah called, then hurried off in the other direction.

A few hours later, Mo was hunched over a sheet of paper in the lunchroom. "Show me one more time."

"It's easy," Jessie said. "All you have to do is . . ."

"Stop saying it's easy or I'm going to slap you," Mo interrupted.

"Fine." Jessie grinned. She drew a horizontal line on the loose-leaf page and began to explain the mathematical concept again.

Hannah plopped down in front of them and listened as Jessie finished the explanation. "We have about thirty questions just like that for homework," Hannah said. "Mr. Lee kept doing examples on the board, and we hardly had any time to work on them."

"I wish I was in your class then," Mo said. "I needed more examples." *Or maybe I need to concentrate better.*

"Call me tonight if you're still having trouble," said Jessie.

Mo exhaled sharply. "Okay. Thanks."

"Are you excited about your big date? Was it sweet when he asked you?" asked Hannah, shifting excitedly from side to side.

Mo was in no mood to explain about the shampoo and alarm clock. It could be funny someday, but not today. Joe was sitting across the lunchroom with Darius and a couple of other guys. "I can't go through with it," Mo said finally.

"What?" asked Hannah.

Mo stood abruptly and with quick, deliberate steps approached Joe's table. "Hi," he said as she drew near.

"Got a second?" Mo said.

"Have a seat," Joe said, then flipped his hair out of his eyes.

When Mo hesitated, he stood up and followed her to an empty table.

"Look, Joe," she began as she sat, "I can't go out with you tomorrow."

"Do you have basketball practice?"

"No, I don't."

"Still hate me for the way I asked you out?"

"No." Mo smiled. "And while we're on the subject, have you told anyone about that?"

"Are you kidding? I feel like a total dork. You haven't either, then?"

"No. I feel stupid for jumping to the wrong conclusion and . . . everything."

They were silent for a few long seconds. "Why don't you want to go?" Joe asked.

Mo shrugged, then looked at the guys sitting at the nearby tables. They were all a bunch of jerks next to Joe. "It's Nathan," she admitted. "He was giving me a hard time about going on a single date instead of a group date."

"Oh," Joe said with understanding. "My dad said something similar, but I was able to convince him that you and I have been friends for so long that, you know, we're cool together."

"I said that too, basically. But Nathan is a tougher sell than your dad, I guess. He kept saying things like 'So you think you're the exception to the rule,' and stuff like that. He really made me mad."

"But— "

"But then I dug out my *Strength of Youth* pamphlet, and it does say something about dating in groups when we're young."

"So if I get a group together, are we back on?"

Mo was drawn to the enthusiasm illuminating his blue eyes. "Of course," she said. His lips spread into a smile. Mo could have sat there in the lunchroom staring at him for the rest of the day.

Joe jumped up and said, "I'll fix it and me and the group will be by to pick you up about 6:40 tomorrow."

"Okay," Mo replied. "I sure hope Nathan's home to see *all* of us off."

She returned to her table and sat with Hannah and Jessie.

"What just happened?" Hannah asked. "And what do you mean, you couldn't go through with it? Did you turn him down?"

"You've been waiting for this," added Jessie.

"The date is on. But Joe and I have decided to make it a group date instead."

Jessie arched a brow. "A group date? I thought you really liked this guy."

"I do," Mo said. Then with more feeling she repeated, "Yeah, I really do. But we shouldn't be single dating. In our church, Jessie, we are told that we are supposed to wait until we are sixteen to date—"

"Yeah, you already told me that," Jessie said. "That's why you've been waiting for like a year to go on a real date with him. Now you're telling me that the 'real' date isn't really 'real' at all?"

Mo shrugged. "It's real, but a group date. A bunch of people out on a date—together."

Jessie huffed. "That doesn't sound like a real date to me."

"It's just a different kind of date," Hannah put in.

"Weird," Jessie muttered, then popped a grape into her mouth.

Before lunch period was over, Joe came to their table with Darius and a boy named Robert. "How would you girls like to join me and my friends for an evening of fun and laughter?"

"Who's asking me out?" Jessie wanted to know.

Darius looked at his feet, and Robert got red in the face. "It's not like that," Joe said evenly. "It's like I was telling these guys. We don't have to be matched up. We're just a group of friends going out on a group date."

"So you can go out with Maury," said Jessie.

Joe shrugged his shoulders. "Yeah, I guess if you want to put it that way."

"It sounds like fun," said Hannah.

"Can you make it?" Joe asked Jessie.

"Of course. I'm kind of glad my friend isn't going to completely desert us on her birthday" —Jessie looked up at Joe with a smirk— "just to go out with some dumb guy."

Joe grinned at her. "Thank you very much. How about if we meet at the birthday girl's house at seven?"

"All the movies start at seven," said Hannah. "Won't we be late?"

"We've made some other plans," Joe said.

A smile crept onto Mo's face. "What is it?"

"Not telling," Joe said.

Jessie cocked her head. "A group date and you're not going to tell us what we're doing? This is a first."

"Don't be so mysterious," Hannah said.

Joe laughed, then said with a smirk, "Dress warm!"

5

Group Date

Hannah and Jessie plopped down on Mo's bed. Mo leaned her face toward the mirror above her dresser. "Are you sure?" she repeated for the fifth time.

"I'm telling you. Leave it alone," said Hannah. "That eyeshadow looks great on you."

Jessie glanced up from the magazine she was flipping through. "It does."

Mo stepped back from the mirror. "But I don't look like me."

Hannah groaned.

"Wash it off if it makes you feel better," Jessie said.

Hannah shot Jessie a look and muttered, "Don't give her that option."

"You look good," Jessie said. "But it's up to you—take off the eyeshadow if you want."

"It's just Joe. What's the big deal, right?" Mo sighed.

"He's super cute," Jessie said matter-of-factly.

"I know!" Mo said with a huge grin. Then the three girls burst out giggling.

"What's Robert like?" Jessie asked once the laughter died out. "I've seen him around but he's not in any of my classes, and he doesn't play sports or stuff like that. What's the deal with him?"

"He's a really nice guy," Mo replied. "I think he plays soccer in the summer."

"Do you think he's cute?" Hannah asked Jessie.

Jessie chomped on her gum a few times. A smile crept up the corners of her lips. Before she had a chance to answer, the doorbell rang and she said, "Sounds like they're here."

"Someone else can get the door," Mo said. Then she frowned at Jessie. "Why did you ask?"

"Just wondered what you thought of him."

"He's cute in a little boy kind of way," Hannah said.

"Little?" Jessie said. "He's taller than Joe, and a lot taller than Darius."

"Darius is taller than I am." Hannah sounded defensive.

Both Mo and Jessie stared at her, all smiles. "He is, is he?" Mo said.

Hannah looked like a deer in the headlights. "Yeah. So I noticed his height? I am totally *not* interested."

"Maury!" Nathan's voice blared down the hallway. "There are some guys here."

Mo rolled her eyes. "I bet he's been out there interrogating them." Jessie and Hannah scampered around the room, finding the jackets they had tossed off. Jessie's was on the bed, but Hannah's had slipped off and was under the straight-back chair.

Mo glanced in the mirror. The eyeshadow looked okay.

The three girls hurried down the hallway into the living room. Standing just inside the doorway, right in front of Nathan and Mom, were Joe, Robert, and Darius, looking totally awkward— and relieved that the interview with Mo's parent and big brother was at an end. Mo grabbed her jacket out of the closet, and the "group daters" hurried out the front door.

"Don't be late," called Nathan.

"Have a good time," Mom added.

Joe fell into step next to Mo. "Happy Birthday, Mo," he said as they stepped onto the sidewalk.

"Does my hair look clean enough?" she said softly with a smirk on her face. "Or should I take a rain check on the date and go wash it?"

Joe laughed. "You look great."

Mo's hair was down for once, hanging straight instead of pulled back into a ponytail. She was wearing an outfit she had saved for this evening, and a cozy black zippered hoodie, a birthday present from Mom. According to Mom, the black was a vibrant contrast with Mo's blond hair and made her skin look silky. It was only partly visible under her winter coat, though.

"Where are we going?" asked Hannah. The little group gathered in a circle on the sidewalk.

Joe cleared his throat. "Your mission, if you choose to accept it, is to take part in a kidnapping."

"Drinking coffee is against your religion but not kidnapping?" Jessie said.

"He needs to be kidnapped," Joe said defensively.

"It's really an act of charity," Darius agreed.

"This way," said Robert, then led the group to the north and out of the Spring Creek section of town. The sun was setting, and the pink tones seemed to reflect on Robert's dark brown hair. He had on a hoodie with a jean jacket over it that was well worn with permanent-looking creases at the elbows. "I'll tell you the story of this poor little guy," Robert said. "He isn't treated very well at all. He works all the time. He never" —Robert looked at each of the girls in turn— "never gets to go out with friends."

"Aww," said Jessie. "Poor guy. Why can't he go out?"

"He's not allowed," said Darius.

"He's been living like this for years," Joe explained. "I see him sometimes, just standing out in his yard."

"Standing there all lonely," added Darius.

"Definitely looks lonely," Joe said.

Mo scowled. "Okay, what is this about, really?"

"It's a kidnapping." Joe transformed his grin into a serious expression. "It's up to us to help him have a good time, for once in his life."

"And if we get caught?" Hannah said, sidestepping a slushy puddle.

"Jail," Robert said dramatically.

"Definite jail time," Darius agreed.

"Well, Mo, your very first date, and there's a chance of jail time." Jessie shook her head at Joe. "You don't want to start out slow or anything, do you, Joe?"

Joe laughed.

In the twilight, the group crossed Main Street and headed into a residential area. Joe reached for Mo's hand. His hand was warm and smooth against hers. Looking straight ahead, she let her fingers intertwine with his.

As they walked, Darius and Jessie bantered about something. A connection, an energy, seemed to flow between Mo's hand and Joe's. He turned toward her. She felt lost in his blue eyes; they were like an expanse of sky she could float through forever. Any awkwardness faded, and they shared a smile.

"Is it on this side of the tracks?" Robert asked, then stopped to wait while Joe and Mo caught up.

The moment of connection passed, and Joe dropped Mo's hand. "Yeah, it's on this side," Joe said. "We have to turn right at the next street."

Joe and Mo took the lead, and the rest of the group followed closely behind. They approached a hedge, and Joe crouched down behind it. The others crouched as well. "This is where he lives," Joe whispered.

"That's President Harris's house," Mo said.

Jessie turned to her. "President? President of what?"

"He's their Church leader," Darius said. "He's like the pastor."

Mo sighed. "President Harris needs rescuing?"

"He's the villain!" Joe said.

"We're supposed to believe that President Harris has a child we've never heard about, chained up in the basement?"

"Something like that," Joe replied.

"You're sure he's not going to get mad?" Robert asked.

"I'm sure," Joe whispered back. "We'll be careful."

"You girls wait here," instructed Darius. "We'll go get him."

"The poor, neglected—" began Mo.

"—oppressed fellow," finished Joe.

The boys scurried around the hedge. Darius wore a tan jacket and was the easiest to keep track of. Soon the other two boys were little more than shadows.

"What are they doing?" whispered Hannah.

"He looks like the hunchback of Notre Dame," Jessie said, pointing at one of the dark shapes that could have been either Joe or Robert.

The boys gathered under the living room window. They were talking in whispers that made their way to the girls as a low hiss. Suddenly, the boys took off at a run. Joe had something under his right arm as he and Robert and Darius took shelter behind the hedge.

"Stop blocking the light," Joe whispered to Robert. "Let them see." In the glow from the streetlight, the kidnapping prize was revealed—a ceramic garden gnome. The little elf-like man had an annoying smile on his frozen face. He wore a red stocking cap and a matching shirt. In one of his hands, he held a hoe.

"Just try to tell me he doesn't look sad," said Joe.

At that, all six of them burst out laughing. "Shh," Joe said, then peeked over the hedge. "So, will you be our accomplices and take this little guy out for a night on the town?"

"It's kind of stealing," said Hannah.

Joe shook his head. "We're going to bring him back, so it's more like we're borrowing him."

"I'm in," said Mo.

"Me too," Hannah and Jessie said in unison.

"Let's get out of here," said Joe with a smile.

Robert shook his head. "Not yet. We have to document the escape, remember."

"How could I forget?" Joe said. He took a camera out of his coat pocket and handed it to Robert, then looked nervously at President Harris's house. "But make it quick or this is going to end before it begins."

Mo glanced over the hedge. The same lights shone from the house, and the front door seemed tightly closed.

"Okay, everybody gather around." Robert raised the camera to take a photo, then lowered it again. "This guy needs a name. Tom? Fred? Barney?"

"Whatever," said Hannah. "It's a garden gnome."

"This is the last thing I was expecting to do tonight," said Jessie with a grin. "So how about something that starts with the last letter of the alphabet. Zack or—what else starts with 'Z'?"

"I like Zack," said Mo.

Joe nodded. "Birthday girl says 'Zack.'"

"Okay then, gather around Zack." Robert lifted the camera into position. "Smile, we are about to give Zack the night of his life."

The flash illuminated the little group in their hiding place. Robert handed the camera to Joe, who slipped it back into his pocket. Then he grabbed Zack, holding him like a football, and said, "Let's go."

For the next hour, they ran around town, snapping pictures with Zack, and laughing a lot. They took a picture of Zack waiting in line at the movie theatre, eating an ice cream cone, and hanging out on a swing at the park.

Finally, Joe checked his watch. "We have to get a picture of Zack on the landing pad."

"My mom says that thing is the biggest waste of money," said Robert.

"No way," said Hannah. "It's cool. St. Paul is the friendliest place in the galaxy. We have a UFO landing pad. Everyone, including aliens, is welcome here."

"Zack has to visit the landing pad," Mo agreed. "His night on the town won't be complete without it."

The little group walked toward Main Street. Robert, who was taking his turn carrying Zack, said in an urgent whisper, "Do you think the cops are looking for him yet?"

"His owner, Mr. Harris, must have called the cops by now and told them his captive has gone missing," said Darius. "But wait, if he's a captive, then Mr. Harris probably *wouldn't* call the cops."

"It's going to be dangerous on Main Street," Mo said. "Zack could be spotted."

"You need to be here," Joe said, guiding Robert so he was walking on the inside, "away from the traffic, and prying eyes. Everyone gather around to shield Zack." They encircled the gnome. "With his team of bodyguards," Joe said loudly, "Zack will have his day!"

Hannah giggled. "Hidden away from misguided strangers who might turn him in."

"We're performing a benevolent act of service . . . sort of," said Hannah.

"Yes, look at his face," Jessie put in. "He's starting to look happier already."

Robert climbed the stairs to the large round platform that was the UFO landing pad. The tourist information center on the left was shaped like a UFO, and it was closed for the day.

"They clear the snow off this thing?" asked Mo as she reached the top.

Robert placed Zack in the center of the disk and said, "Zack, welcome to Earth!"

They took his picture, first alone and then with the group. The selfie didn't get enough of the background, so Joe and Robert each snapped a picture so everyone would have a chance to be in the shot.

Then the six friends settled around the gnome. Joe checked his watch and looked out at the road. "Now, there's one more thing that Zack has never done that he really needs to experience. He's never been to a birthday party."

Suddenly, Mark Parker, Joe's little brother, came up the steps of the landing pad. He was carrying a square foil baking dish with candles in it—sixteen, Mo guessed. Mark handed the cake to Joe, then fished around in his coat pocket and handed Joe a pack of matches. "Happy Birthday, Maury," Mark said before he ran back down the steps and got into the waiting mini-van. The van honked twice as a greeting and then pulled away from the curb.

"Your mom knew you were kidnapping a gnome tonight?" Darius said.

Joe smiled. "Are you kidding? She'd have my head. No. She only knows I wanted to serve Mo her birthday cake on the UFO landing pad. That's why I had Mark deliver the cake. Now, nobody laugh. I made the cake myself, and icing it wasn't easy."

It looked like part of the top layer of the cake had lifted and become part of the chocolate icing. A knife was tucked in at the side of the pan. Joe lit the candles, and Hannah led the group in a loud rendition of "Happy Birthday." Joe cut the cake and gave the first piece to Maury, and the second to Zack. Darius re-lit a candle and stuck it in Zack's serving of cake. Robert took the picture as Joe dished out cake for the rest of the friends, who sat cross legged in a circle.

Joe looked over at Mo with a lopsided smile. "Happy Sweet Sixteen, Mo."

They ate cake, talked, and laughed. Eventually, Joe looked at his watch and exclaimed. "Oh no! We better get a move on or we won't get the gnome back to President Harris's and get Mo home on time."

Darius chuckled. "You don't want to deal with her big brother?" Joe gave him a look. Then Darius turned to Hannah. "Do you have a big brother?"

"Yes," she answered.

"Too bad," Jessie said with a smirk.

The group set off. With even more stealth than the actual kidnapping, Mo and Joe snuck up to their branch president's house. The outside light suddenly blazed to life. "Whatcha doing out here?" shouted a deep voice.

Joe grabbed Mo's hand, and they sprinted to the flowerbed with their heads down. "Hey, do I know you?" yelled President Harris. He came out on the front step. "This is private property!"

The slap of sneakers on the sidewalk drew Mo's attention. The rest of the group was running down the street. "Joe?"

"Don't look at him," Joe whispered, then replaced the gnome in the front flowerbed as President Harris came down the steps. Joe and Mo took off after their friends and didn't look back.

At the corner, they caught up with the others. "Let's take the alley," Joe said. Keeping to the shadows, they made it back to Mo's house. "You're a pretty good accomplice," Joe told her.

"Thank you, oh mastermind. I really thought we were going to get caught." Mo brought her hand to her throat. Then she looked at her watch. "Looks like we'll avoid the wrath of Nathan."

"Good!" Joe said seriously.

"She's not going to turn into a pumpkin," said Robert.

"I just don't want to make anybody mad," said Joe. "I mean, I might want to ask her out again . . . sometime."

Jessie huffed. "That's no surprise."

"Who would've thought," Robert put in. "I think we should all go out again . . . sometime."

"It *is* a group date," Jessie said.

Robert nodded. "True. So how about if you girls plan something next time?"

The three girls caught each other's eyes. "Okay," they agreed.

6

Not Nathan's Girlfriend

"So, then I gave them a look and called out, 'Don't be late,' and you should have seen his eyes. They must have doubled in size!" Nathan chuckled, then took a big gulp of his root beer.

"You're not very nice," scolded Sarah, the girl across from him in the booth.

"Hey, I'm the big brother. It's like my job."

Sarah pushed her dark bangs out of her eyes. "Just what is the job description of a big brother?"

"Well, besides terrorizing any guy who wants to take out his sister . . . I guess it's stealing the remote control, eating huge amounts of food, giving rides to young boys' soccer practices" —Nathan rolled his eyes— "and making fun of chick flicks. That about sums it up."

"I'm glad you're not my brother."

Nathan winked at her. "I'm glad I'm not your brother, too." He dropped his eyes to the order of fries on the tray between them. "I'll get more ketchup," he said as beads of sweat formed on the back of his neck. He hadn't winked at anyone, ever.

Sarah had worked at A&W almost as long as Nathan had. Now that he also worked for the steel company, he only took a couple of shifts each week at the restaurant. He would have looked for something that paid a little better if it weren't for Sarah. He had been crazy about her for over a year. Today they had joked around during their shift, and he finally got up the courage to ask her to have a soda with him after work.

It was senseless, really. He would be leaving on his mission in eight or nine months. He would have left already but had to earn more money to pay for it. But he couldn't leave town for two years and never ask Sarah out. If she said no, then she said no. At least he would stop being ruled by his fear of rejection.

He got the ketchup and returned to the table. The overhead lights in the dining room brought out the auburn highlights in Sarah's long, dark hair. She looked beautiful, even with a bit of "hat head" from the baseball cap that was part of their uniform.

"Do you think you got enough?" Sarah laughed as Nathan placed three paper containers of ketchup on the table. "We have six fries left."

Nathan shrugged. "Eat up." He dipped a long fry thoroughly in ketchup. "Don't worry, I'll eat most of it. It's part of what big brothers do, remember? Eat lots."

"You take this big brother stuff very seriously, don't you?"

She was grinning but Nathan didn't smile. "I do," he said. "Actually, I really do."

Most of the other customers had left the restaurant, so it was quiet.

"Since the fire . . . " Sarah began. "Well, you've been a lot more serious about everything, it seems." She fiddled with the pearl ring on her right hand. "I'm sorry about your dad. I know I've said it before." They sat in silence for a moment with Nathan only nodding his head. Eventually, Sarah continued, "It was really nice to see you goofing around today like you used to."

"It felt good. But have I really been so different?" Nathan could see the changes in Maury since their dad had died, especially her drive to succeed in basketball like it was the end-all of her existence. He could see the changes in Bailey, how she seemed to need acceptance so desperately. He could see the changes in his mom as she took on the role of breadwinner. But Nathan hadn't noticed any changes in Jordy or himself.

"Let's just say it was nice to have a cheery boyfriend today." Nathan's jaw dropped, and somehow he still managed to miss his mouth. The ketchup drenched fry made contact with his cheek.

Sarah smirked and put on a false innocent expression. "What, soldier? Rough fight? Need a Band-Aid?"

"What?"

She picked up a napkin and handed it to him, pointing at the right side of his face. "You look like you're bleeding. Nathan, the returning hero of some great battle."

Nathan dropped the fry onto the plastic orange tray, accepted the paper napkin, and wiped his cheek.

Sarah picked up another napkin and leaned toward him until she was frighteningly close. She dabbed at a spot he had missed. He had never felt so flustered in his life. He had felt abandoned, he had felt sorrow, and he had felt plenty of guilt, but this was a new emotion, and there was only one good word for it—flustered. "Would you care to . . . how about if you . . . what did you mean by that?" he managed to stutter.

Sarah smiled. "If you raise your eyebrows any higher they'll disappear into your hairline. And I think I should warn you, that's one of those faces mothers warn you about, the kind that will stay that way."

"But did you just call me—?"

"You're still doing it," Sarah said. "Do you want to look perpetually surprised? Sometimes I see them, the little old ladies with their super-high eyebrows. People think they've had facelifts with a little too much lift, but the truth is they just made that face you're making a little too long, and presto! Shocked, surprised, and very energetic eyebrows for life."

Nathan consciously relaxed his facial muscles.

"Much better." Sarah picked up one of the remaining fries and dipped it in the ketchup container. "Do you think that's enough?"

Nathan nodded and suddenly realized his eyebrows were raising again as he tried to come up with a sentence that wouldn't sound like a seven-year-old on a playground asking the pretty girl on the swing to be his girlfriend. The elevator music being pumped into the dining area was a disco hit from the seventies, "Stayin' Alive," by the Bee Gees. It seemed somewhat fitting. Here he was in a fast-food restaurant with Sarah Wonderful Marshall, worried about how he could ask her out on an away-from-the-Dub date, and she was saying she was already his girlfriend. Heck yeah, he was stayin' alive—in fact, he was flying. Baffled, but flying.

"You seem shocked that I called you my boyfriend," said Sarah, eventually.

Nathan caught his eyebrows on their way into his hairline. "Well, I guess I was surprised to hear that."

"Don't you want to be my boyfriend anymore?"

"Anymore? I didn't know I was."

"Don't be silly. Of course you are. You have been for months."

"I really like you, Sarah, but I'm starting to think you're a little loopy. We've never been on a real date."

"Haven't we?"

Nathan looked into her beautiful blue eyes and saw more than he had ever seen there before. He had noticed the caring in them as they had talked about his family one night when he drove her home from work. They had sat in his car in the glow of the streetlights for over an hour. Another time they discussed their plans for the future. Sarah had one more year of high school and was very bright, but she hadn't a clue what she wanted to do. Nathan told her about his plan to serve a mission, something she didn't understand but respected. They often took their breaks together and had joked around in the staff room, once so loudly that the owner asked them to keep it down because they could be heard not only in the kitchen but out in the dining room. *Maybe she's saying all those talks were dates . . .*

Actually, they were better than dates. Dinner-and-a-movie type dates revealed only pieces of someone's personality, their values, or their soul. It was like Nathan and Sarah had been on dozens of dates. Maybe hundreds.

"We've been on lots of dates," he admitted, then smiled sheepishly. "I just didn't know."

"I was afraid of that." Sarah drank her root beer until the straw was slurping more air than soda, the noise that always brought a stern look from Nathan's mother when they were in a restaurant. She set the cup on the table like she was making a point.

"I was just about to ask you out," Nathan said.

"I thought so. And it kind of seemed like you've never done it before."

"I haven't," Nathan replied, then hurried to add, "a technicality, granted, but I haven't." He let his eyes drop to the table. There was one fry left in the cardboard container. "I wanted to but, I guess I'm kind of a coward."

Sarah shook her head slowly. "You are a hero, Nathan Matheson. Nothing short of a hero."

He raised his eyes and they locked with hers. She wasn't joking around or being sarcastic. And she was so wrong. The guilt was always with him, sometimes fierce, sometimes a dull ache. Now it flared like a gasoline-doused bonfire with a torch thrown on top. "You shouldn't say that."

"I admire you so much. The night of the fire—"

"You don't know anything about that night. I'm no hero, Sarah." With that, Nathan slipped out of the booth. "And I'm not your boyfriend." He turned away, and almost as an afterthought asked, "Do you need a ride today?"

Sarah shook her head.

"See ya," he mumbled. It wasn't right to walk out on her like that, and he was messing things up, but he couldn't stop. They didn't know each other dozens of dates worth after all, not if Sarah Marshall thought he was a hero.

7

Messages for Nathan

A week later, Nathan went for a run. Feeling enclosed in the stillness of the quiet town, he quickened his pace. The slap of his shoes against the sidewalk seemed to be swallowed by the night. Swallowed in the silence. He felt like an astronaut, the space around him a black hole sucking in the sights, sounds, emotions. He was alone in the vastness. If he screamed, no one would hear.

And yet he knew he wasn't alone. He had a work to do and he heard the words in his mind with such clarity they rang in his ears. *Keep going. Build endurance. Build strength.* Nathan quickened his pace again. The stitch in his side wailed a protest, but he pushed through it.

He had clocked his route on his car odometer a few days ago and was surprised to find he was running almost eleven miles now.

His lungs burned. He focused on his breathing. *In and out. Keep it controlled. In and out.* He had to be ready. *In and out.* People would be counting on him. "What people?" he whispered aloud. "Sarah?"

She was so lovely. Nathan focused on the image of her smiling face. He left Main Street and rhythmically moved along the sidewalk. There was lamplight in one of the homes, and no telltale blue of a television. He liked that. The people in the house were probably reading, talking, or laughing.

The vision of Sarah's smile faded, replaced with the image of flames licking up the living room curtains. As Nathan ran, the evening air stung the back of his throat—like smoke. He started to cough. The energy drained from his legs. He walked and coughed and eventually swallowed. It tasted like smoke.

"We're not dating. She's crazy," he huffed. Even before he finished the words he knew it wasn't true. Sarah was wonderful.

She had been wide-eyed and hurt when he left her at the A&W. He had spent the night tossing and turning and mentally composing an apology that would help them be friends again. They had worked together twice since then. The first day he had almost apologized. When he had arrived for his shift, she was already at the stainless-steel table, mechanically assembling teen burgers. Nathan walked up behind her with the rehearsed speech fresh in his mind, but the words left him as he got closer. He was imagining what her long hair would feel like under his hand when she either sensed him there or caught sight of him and turned. "Oh," she said in surprise.

He couldn't very well begin his apology with "I like your hair," so he stood there like an idiot under the stares of his coworkers and this wonderful girl. After what seemed like an eternity, Sarah smiled and said, "Hi, Nathan."

He mumbled some sort of greeting and turned and walked away. Later in the shift, Sarah spoke to him again. Within a few minutes, she put him at ease, and it was as if the scene the other night had never happened. Nothing was said about it, even though Nathan tried several times to remember the speech he had rehearsed. What had seemed perfect in the late-night hours now seemed fake and corny. Sarah deserved the truth, but he couldn't give it to her. So he gave her nothing.

The shift had ended with a polite exchange—"Have a good-night," and "See you on Thursday."

Even if they had been dating, they definitely weren't now.

Nathan cleared his throat and began to run again. Maury might not like it, but he was going to keep her and Joe at arm's length. He didn't know Joe well enough to actually trust him, and it was obvious that Nathan had intimidated him the night of Maury's birthday. Nathan would be doing it for her own good.

When he got to Lagasse Park on Lakeshore Drive, the air was cooler, blowing over Upper Therein Lake. Suddenly, a dark figure rose from one of the benches and came toward Nathan with brisk steps, then broke into a run. The person was tall and the directness of his approach was alarming. Just as Nathan had decided to change course and head up one of the streets that would take him back toward Main, he recognized the runner approaching him.

"Nathan," called Joe Parker.

"Oh, Joe. Hey," Nathan said, gradually coming to a stop.

"Is it okay if I run with you? I wanted to talk to you but didn't want Mo to know."

"Sure," Nathan said.

They ran at a nice relaxed pace. It was enjoyable to run without the constant push to go farther and faster. After a few minutes of silence, he said, "Okay, Joe, what is it?"

"Well," Joe panted, "it's about Mo, of course." Joe was an athlete and it was basketball season, but he seemed to be having trouble keeping up. "I mean Maury." It was too dark to be sure, but Joe's face seemed to be turning red.

"Everyone knows you call her Mo," said Nathan.

"Oh yeah, I guess so. I know you worry about her," he said, almost out of breath. "And with her old enough to date now—"

"Yeah," Nathan prodded.

"Well . . ."

It occurred to Nathan that the single word was all Joe could get out at the pace he was forced to keep. Nathan slowed.

About half a minute later, Joe continued, "There are guys I wouldn't want my sister to go out with either. If I had a sister, that is."

"Uh-huh," said Nathan. He'd slipped back into his former pace, his training pace as he sometimes referred to it, even though he didn't know what he was training for. He slowed again for Joe's sake.

"Well, I'm not one of those guys, Nathan." Joe's voice was strained. He reached out and grabbed Nathan's forearm, and they slowed and then stopped. Joe placed his hands on his knees and greedily sucked in oxygen. "You're in amazing shape," he said.

Nathan chuckled. "Thanks."

After a moment Joe said, "I want Mo to be happy. I really care about her."

"She has a lot of life choices ahead of her, Joe. I don't want you to get in the way."

"I want her to have what she wants from life, too."

"And what if that isn't you, after a while?"

Joe frowned. "Huh?"

"I see a lot of guys go to extremes to hang on to a girlfriend when it would be better to just let her go."

"I hope we . . . that she . . . will always want to be with me . . . but . . . I won't be pushy."

Nathan nodded. "Glad to hear it. But that's easy to say and harder to do if the person you like wants to go in a different direction."

Joe swallowed hard. "Her happiness comes first."

"And if she wants to move on?"

Joe hesitated as though imagining it, then slowly said, "I'll back off."

Nathan looked at him hard. "Glad to hear it. But I still expect you two to date in groups."

Joe managed a smile. "I know. Well, later," he said and waved a farewell in Nathan's direction.

Resuming his running pace, Nathan called out over his shoulder, "See ya later, Joe."

Nathan turned right at the end of Lakeshore Drive. He was more than halfway through his run. He felt great. That little Joe

Parker was an okay kid. And not that little. Nathan had been afraid when he saw a strange man running toward him. *Man? And good guy or not, Maury is barely sixteen.* It was not the time for steady dating. It was only one date so far, but it was clear that those two really liked each other and this would be the first of many dates. But the kid had put Nathan's mind at ease, and he would stop trying to strike fear into the heart of Joe Parker. Besides, Maury had listened to Nathan and was doing group dates instead of single dating.

Nathan could plant one more thought in her mind and see if it took root. He'd ease into this advice. A little tact could go a long way.

What would Nate Mathews say? Nathan smiled. That was his pen name for the column he secretly wrote for the local newspaper. He had a lot more time to plan his words when he wrote. Things seemed to flow. He could cut to the quick and eliminate babble. In speaking, he seemed to babble constantly — more with Sarah than anyone else.

8

Six Cooks

"Let me see the recipe, again," said Hannah as she sat at the island in Mo's kitchen. Mo handed her the page they had printed off the Internet.

The doorbell rang.

"Why did we choose something so ambitious?" Hannah said. She perused the paper as Mo went to answer the door.

"There are six cooks," Mo said over her shoulder. She turned the handle and opened the door. There was Joe, holding a grocery bag in each hand. In the frame of the doorway, he looked like a painting titled *Honey, I'm Home*. Her heart did a little fluttery thing.

At the sound of a deep-throated *umph*, Mo looked past him. Robert and Darius were standing on the snow-covered lawn. Robert got Darius in a chokehold, but he pulled Robert's arm off and shoved him several feet. Their faces were intense but not angry.

"What's with them?" Mo asked.

Joe shrugged, and then a smirk lit up his features. "I'd call it ego sparing."

"Your ego doesn't need to spar?"

He walked in and Mo took the bags from him. He pulled off his boots. "Oh no. They already know I'm the alpha male." Joe and Mo shared a smile, and she couldn't remember a happier moment.

Seconds later, she was calling out the door, "It's too cold to leave the door open. Come in when you've worn off some testosterone."

"Huh?" Robert said. Then he and Darius jogged up the steps. Jessie followed from out of Mo's sightline.

"I make great stir-fries," said Darius as he walked into the kitchen.

Hannah waved the recipe. "This is a lot more advanced than a stir fry."

They unpacked the vegetables that Joe brought. Hannah got the chicken breasts out of the fridge and set them on the island.

Mo grabbed the cheese, crackers, and spices, then said, "I have to tie my hair back."

"How come?" asked Robert.

"I've learned I get a lot less complaints of 'There's a hair in my food'" —she removed an imaginary hair from a plate— "if I put my hair in a ponytail before I cook."

Darius looked grossed out. "Fantastic idea then!"

Jordy and Nathan entered the kitchen. "If you want to make a little extra," said Nathan."

"You already ate," Mo said.

"Spaghetti," Nathan replied as though it was hardly worth mentioning.

"Can I help?" Jordy asked.

Nathan smiled smugly. "Good idea. He's a great helper."

"Another time," Mo told Jordy.

"Aw, come on," he complained.

"Nathan!" said Mo, looking at him for support. He had planned this, obviously.

"We'll play video games," Nathan told Jordy. "And they can slave in a hot kitchen if they want."

Mo's little brother smiled and followed Nathan.

She led the girls to the bathroom and handed ponytail elastics to her friends. "This is going to be so good," Mo said, putting her hair in a high ponytail.

"Robert smells so good," whispered Jessie. She made a messy bun in her hair and turned to see it from the side. "I don't know if it's deodorant or cologne, but it's nice."

"How did you do that?" asked Hannah, admiring Jessie's hair. "And so fast. It looks good."

"Thanks. The last time I put the pony around I tuck up the ends like this." Jessie demonstrated how to tuck in the hair.

"We're going to practice this another time," said Hannah.

Mo grabbed a lip gloss from the cupboard and put some on.

"Joe's looking good tonight, too," Jessie commented. "I haven't sniffed him, but he looks nice."

Mo laughed as they left the bathroom together.

The guys were gathered around the island. "If you're finally ready," said Robert, "let's get started."

Jessie tilted her head. "Perfection takes time."

"This return date has been a long time coming," said Darius.

"You hang out with basketball players," Joe said apologetically. "And this is basketball season."

Hannah removed the plastic wrap from the package of chicken breasts. "We have to flatten these," she said, taking charge.

Soon everyone had a job. Amid the sound of the little wooden mallet banging against the chicken, Joe washed vegetables and Darius cut them. "Those look like they belong in a stir fry," joked Joe, looking over his shoulder.

Mo placed a stack of soda crackers on a cutting board. Jessie rolled them with a rolling pin, then dumped the crumbs into a bowl, while Mo added spices for the breading.

"They're not flattening," said Robert. The chicken breasts were still thick between sheets of waxed paper. "Are you sure this is supposed to work?"

"Let me try," Joe said. He pounded on the chicken for a couple of minutes. "It's harder than the recipe makes it sound."

Everyone took a turn pounding the chicken, and when that didn't work very well, Mo said, "Let's try the rolling pin."

"This is a little more work than the last time we prepared food together," Joe said, meeting Mo's eyes. He stirred the mushroom sauce in the little pot, then dumped it over the vegetables in a casserole dish.

"When?" Mo said.

"It was just cheese, crackers, and fruit, I believe."

"Oh, yeah," said Mo. "Sister Andrews, at the Edmonton service project. Yeah. Why didn't we do something spectacular like this?"

"We were . . . lazy." Joe shook his head as though disappointed in her.

"Except we were laying sod, and Sister Andrews had morning sickness that apparently lasted all day."

"Yeah, but we totally could have made something impressive."

Mo looked at the six chicken breasts. "That's as flat as they're going to get."

"Now a slice of Swiss cheese on each one," Hannah said, demonstrating. "We roll them and stick toothpicks in to hold them together."

"They are so slippery." Jessie giggled as the meat slipped out of her fingers time after time. Finally, Robert held it while she used nine toothpicks to hold hers together.

"Stab it again," Joe said, laughing. "I think it needs one more."

Mo smiled at their banter, but this was a group date, and she missed feeling singled out by Joe.

They dipped the chicken bundles in a bowl of beaten eggs, and then rolled the chicken in the breading.

"They look so pretty," said Jessie.

"You mean yummy," said Robert.

"No, they look beautiful."

"Beauty doesn't matter when it comes to food," Robert said. "Either something is good or it's not. Taste is the only thing that matters."

"That's not true." Jessie fluttered her fingers in a large circle. "It's the whole experience."

Robert bumped her with his hip. "Let's stop admiring them and get them in the oven so I can experience it . . . with my mouth."

Jessie laughed. "Only if you'll admit they are pretty."

"No way. Not even cute."

"You're so stubborn," Jessie said, bumping him back.

Suddenly, Robert grabbed her around the waist from behind. Her feet left the floor and she squealed. After a moment she cried, "Put me down." Their laughter filled the room.

Mo glanced at Joe. This reminded her of the day after the service project in Edmonton. Joe hadn't done anything remotely like this since. *Maybe we're an old, boring couple now. Maybe the spontaneous spark is gone.*

Robert set Jessie down. *They* were the cute couple of the group.

"I'm so hungry," said Robert.

Jessie smirked at him. "Your cute food will be done soon."

Darius put the chicken on a greased cookie sheet and slipped it into the oven next to the vegetable casserole that had been cooking a while.

"I have the pictures from Zack's excursion," Joe said.

All six friends went into the family room, where Joe removed a stack of photos from his coat pocket. There were shots of Zack at the theatre, and the park, and the UFO landing pad. Mo laughed along with the others.

"What should we do with them?" asked Darius.

"I was thinking we could plant them in places President Harris will find them," said Joe.

"We could write little notes on the back," Hannah suggested. "'Don't Fence Me In,' or 'Take Me out to the Ball Game.'"

Robert laughed. "On the landing pad one, we could write, I'm looking for my own kind."

"The chicken won't be done for forty-five minutes," Mo said. She brought pens and they tucked them in their pockets, put on their winter coats, and piled into Joe's family's car. He drove to President Harris's house. It was already dark. Mo and Hannah snuck around, putting photos in the groove of the windowpane of the storm doors at the front and back of the house. They met their other friends out front.

"I hope it doesn't snow tonight," Joe said, slipping a couple of photos under the windshield wipers of President Harris's car. "Dad has a key to the church meetinghouse on this ring. We could slide one under the door of his office."

Mo nodded. "That's great. He won't be expecting that."

"I feel bad breaking into your church," said Darius.

"It's not breaking in," Robert said, laughing. "We have a key."

They went in and Joe pulled out the remaining pictures. Mo picked out the one of Zack with an ice cream cone. "How about 'Who's in charge of refreshments?'"

"That's great," Hannah replied.

Joe handed Mo a pen. She wrote the sentence, and they slipped the photo under his office door.

"Our timer's going to ring soon," Hannah said. "We better get going."

Dinner was inhaled in less than twenty minutes.

9

Mo's First Job

Mo had written a list of basketball camps on a piece of paper next to the computer. She added the University of Alberta summer camp to the top. It would be the best . . . and also the most expensive. Some of the girls on her team had said it would be nice to have their lives back when the season ended. Basketball wasn't in the way of Mo's life—it was her life. No, basketball and Joe were her life.

The coach had suggested that the players go to a camp this summer if they could. "It would really help us have a strong team next year," he said. Mo's dad had been the coach before he was killed in the house fire.

If all the other girls went and Mo didn't, she'd fall behind. Maybe they would improve so much that she wouldn't make the team next year. A ripple of panic moved through her. Practicing by herself was only going to get her so far. She had to go to a camp. But it cost hundreds of dollars. Mo hated to ask her mother, who often complained about the price of gas, and how on the days when she had to go to her office in Edmonton, she hardly made anything. There were four hours of driving, as well as eating out at least one meal because she had to leave early and get home so late.

Mo found her mother in her bedroom with a library book. "Can I talk to you?" Mo asked.

Her mom took off her reading glasses and set the book beside her on the bed. "What's up?" She patted the bed beside her.

Mo sat with one leg bent. "I've been looking at basketball camps for this summer."

"Summer? That's a long way away."

"Yeah, but I need to plan now." Mo handed the list to her mother. "I think the U of A camp will be the best by far."

Mom whistled, no doubt looking at the prices Mo had written beside the dates and locations.

Mo's heart sank in her chest. "That's with accommodations."

"I should hope so." Mom looked up. "I bet Nathan could give you a lot of pointers, and you improved so much just practicing over at the park last year." She put a warm hand on Mo's shoulder. Mo nodded, not trusting herself to speak past the lump in her throat. "I can kick in a couple of hundred dollars, maybe three," Mom said, "but if you want to go to an expensive camp like this, you're going to have to get a job and pay for a good chunk of it yourself."

"Okay, I will. Thanks, Mom." Mo leaned in and they hugged.

Mo went out to the living room and took *The St. Paul Journal* out of the magazine rack, then settled into the recliner.

Nathan came out of the kitchen eating a granola bar. He sat on the couch and said, "Hey."

"Hi." Mo was reading through the classifieds. "They're hiring at McDonalds."

"McDonalds? I didn't know you were looking for a job. It's about time, ya lazy kid."

Mo rolled her eyes. "I was checking out a basketball camp at the University of Alberta this summer. It's pretty expensive, so Mom said I need to earn some of the money. I should make enough if I start working right away."

Nathan smiled. "Why not apply at A&W?"

"I could," Mo said reluctantly.

"But?"

She shrugged. Working next to him for hours on end? He was an okay brother, but he would be always looking over her shoulder to make sure she was doing everything right. That would get on her nerves. Besides, everyone there would think of her as Nathan's little sister. Mo wanted to earn some money and feel grown up. She wouldn't feel grown up if she was in her big brother's shadow all the time.

"McDonalds is kind of like the enemy to us Dubbers," Nathan joked. "I can't have you working for the 'other side.' Literally. It's almost exactly on the other side of Main Street."

"McDonald's has an ad, though," Mo said, not commenting on the restaurants' rivalry.

Nathan laughed. "It's the tiniest McDonalds I've ever seen."

"And A&W is so huge?"

"We have seating for more than twelve."

"So McDonalds is a better place to work—less to clean." Mo raised an eyebrow at him.

Nathan smiled. "A part-time job will be good—then you can't date Joe every weekend."

"Oh brother."

"You and Joe and your friends made that dinner the other night, like a bunch of miniature married couples." He cleared his throat. "How was the food?"

"Pretty good. Darius put way too much pepper in the vegetable casserole but we ate it anyway. The chicken was great, though."

"Who made that?"

"All of us, really. Quite a lot of the cheese oozed out, but they were yummy. Maybe I'll make them again sometime so you can try them. It was called chicken saltimbocca or something like that. I kept the recipe."

"So do you have any other dates—you know, with any other guys?"

Frowning, Mo placed the newspaper on the coffee table. "No."

"Well, just remember, you shouldn't be steady dating."

"Steady dating?"

"Yeah."

"I've been on two dates in my life. Both group dates, in case you didn't notice. I hardly think I'm 'steady dating.'"

"Well, twice in a row with the same guy . . . " Nathan let the sentence hang in the air.

"Nathan. You. Are. Crazy."

"Just something to think about," he said nonchalantly. He picked up the newspaper from the table and opened it to the local sports section.

One week later, Mo stood behind the counter at McDonalds with a view of the A&W across the street. She was dressed in an ugly brown uniform and smelled of grease. Her fingers were sticky from a mayonnaise bottle that needed to be washed. She got a cloth and wiped it down. It was almost time for her break. What a way to spend a Saturday. *Think of the money,* she thought. *Think of a university basketball camp.*

A few minutes later, she collapsed in the staff room with a burger and an order of onion rings. She wanted to slip off her sneakers, but the floor looked greasy.

Ken, the manager, peeked his head in the staff room. "I'd like you to take over the deep fryer after your break, Maury. Garrett will show you what to do before he leaves, okay?"

"Okay." There couldn't be a hotter spot to work in this place. This was Mo's third day at work. The first shift had been a four-hour stretch where she filled drinks almost nonstop, and the second had been the same. So far today she had made burgers.

After her break, she reported to the deep fryers. Garrett was a year older than Mo and very cute. His light-brown hair stuck out at odd angles as if he had just gotten out of bed.

"Hot over here," she said.

Garrett laughed. "Just wait." His eyebrows waved up and down like they were bouncing at the end of a yo-yo. "Imagine what it's like in here in July. Oh, and take a look at this." He turned his right arm to show her his elbow, which had a crisscross of white lines. "From the fry baskets," he explained. "I fondly refer to them as my 'Mcburns.'" Garrett gave Mo a friendly smile.

He showed her how full to fill the baskets with frozen French fries and how to set the timers for the fries, chicken, or fish. As the hot oil started to bubble everything to a golden brown, Garrett asked, "Where did you work before here?"

"Nowhere," Mo said.

"Really? This is your first job? I've been here since I turned fourteen. You, my girl, have lived a very cushy life, but that's about to change."

Mo didn't want to get into a discussion about loss and house fires, so she ignored Garrett's comment. The fryer timer went off, so she pulled the basket from the oil and shook it off before emptying the food into the metal bin. "Do you have a lot of money saved?" she asked as Garrett filled fry boxes with an open-ended metal scoop.

"Ha! Are they paying you more than they're paying me?"

"I don't think that's possible."

"Good ol' minimum wage."

"But you've been working for years."

"So I'll have spending money."

"Oh. I'm saving for a basketball camp."

"Camp?" Garrett laughed. "Do you climb in your tent at night and sleep with your hand on a basketball?"

Mo arched her eyebrow and looked at him sideways. "Uh, no. Only if I fall asleep during a drill. I'll be staying in a campus dorm."

"Hardly sounds like camping to me. Do you at least get to roast marshmallows?"

Mo laughed. "I don't think we're talking about the same kind of camp."

"So you're going to work, work, work, and then spend it on a basketball camp?" Garrett shook his head.

"What do you do with your money?" Mo asked.

"Go to movies. Eat out with friends. I'm living the good life."

Garrett had a carefree attitude as though life wasn't really such a serious business. His attitude was kind of contagious.

Later, he brought up the subject again. "So, Miss Focused, you're never going to blow money on movies?" His bangs were a little too long, and he was constantly flipping them out of his eyes.

"I might," Mo replied. "But not very often. I have a goal. A good one."

Garrett touched her shoulder. "It's cool. Very cool." His serious tone was quickly replaced with his regular one. "And speaking of cool, what do you think of this?"

He lowered one shoulder to the beat of the song barely audible in the kitchen. Then he spun and held out his hand to her. "My new dance move. Do you like it?"

"It's great, but I wouldn't do it this close to the deep fryers."

"Good idea. Except that I'm so sure on my feet, there's not much risk of becoming a dancer-mc-nugget."

The hour and a half Mo spent with Garrett flew by. After he left the restaurant, time seemed to drag. She smiled inside as she replayed their conversation in her head. He was a little crazy, spinning around deep fryers, but he was a lot of fun.

The buzzing of the fryers brought Mo's mind back to the present. *Twenty-five more minutes,* she thought after dumping the fries into the metal bin. *Almost free.*

10

An Overheard Conversation

Nathan finished his shift at A&W and searched the restaurant for Sarah. Her shift ended at the same time as his. "Is Sarah in there?" he asked one of the girls exiting the girls' changing room.

"No. She left already."

Nathan went out in the restaurant seating area. She wasn't there, either. Maybe she had raced home without saying goodbye to her boyfriend.

He went out the main door and wandered toward the employee entrance at the back. He stepped around where the snow had drifted. There Sarah was, sitting at the picnic table with her back to him, talking on her cell phone. Then she pulled the phone away from her ear, touched the screen, and set the phone on the table beside her. She took a brush out of her bag and brushed her hair. "Well, I've completely freaked him out, there's no two ways about it," Sarah said.

"There's a good possibility," the other person said matter-of-factly. Sarah had the call on speaker phone.

"He thinks I'm a nut," she said.

"You *are* a nut, Sarah."

"Carly!"

"It's best he knows that about you. He should know *something* that's real."

Nathan cringed. He should let her know he was there, but he wanted to hear more. He stepped closer to the building.

"I'm not trying to give you a hard time," said this Carly person. "But I'll have to admit, you probably scared this guy—big time. The question is, what are you going to do about it? And are you sure you want him after this? I mean if a guy can't even figure out that he has a girlfriend . . . "

"All right. You've made your point." There was silence for a moment. "Look, Nathan is fantastic and I think he likes me." Nathan held his breath as Sarah continued. "He was asking me out before I interrupted him and told him we were already dating."

"Yeah. So, what are you going to do? Apologize?"

"How can I apologize? I didn't say anything that wasn't the truth. Does everything have to be so literal? Does he have to say, 'Sarah, would you like to go on a date with me?' before we actually have one?"

"I don't know. You ask hard questions." Carly chuckled. "Are you making cookies tonight?"

"Nothing you'd like."

"Bring me some tomorrow?"

"All right."

"Look, just keep being yourself. Nathan will either see how terrific you are, or he'll miss out on the best girl he could go out with. Then you'll have to make some other guy happy. How bad would that be?"

Nathan stopped short and pressed his back against the wall.

Sarah gave a loud sigh.

"Yeah, I know." Carly paused to cough. "Pretty bad."

"I really like him. It might even be love."

"Word of advice—don't tell him that."

"I know. Hey, thanks for listening . . . again. We should psychoanalyze you next. How about it?"

"Sounds like fun, but I better go do a workout. I have a bunch of delicious cookies coming to school tomorrow with my name on them. The soft chocolate ones?"

"Yeah."

"An even dozen should be enough."

"See ya tomorrow."

Nathan came around the corner at a quick pace. Sarah shifted on the picnic table. She was talking about him, and she had used the L-word. His chest was full, as though there wasn't room for air in his lungs. *Act cool. You didn't hear any of that.*

"There you are," he said, approaching her. "Aren't you cold out here?"

"A little," she admitted, then finished putting her hair in a bun of some sort and stood up.

"Do you want a hot chocolate?" Nathan asked. She nodded, and together they walked back into the restaurant. Once they had their drinks, they settled into a back booth. There was a television in the high corner. Nathan's back was to it, but a documentary of some sort was on. He turned to look. Several sweaty but invigorated-looking men on a pontoon boat were talking about needing protection. Protection from what or for what wasn't clear, but it would be a good excuse to move over and sit by Sarah.

"They look intense," he said, craning his neck. Sarah scooted over to make room for him on her side of the booth.

"My parents always watch shows like this," Sarah said. "They all seem to want to bring despair and outrage to their viewers. If you believed them all, the world is a doomed planet on a predestined course to destruction."

Nathan nodded. "We should be informed, though."

"I like the nature programs on this station. The animals have amazing stories of instinct and survival. Unfortunately, at the end, there's usually a scientist talking about how man has ruined the earth for some species and how if we don't smarten up we will no longer have the wonderful animals we just — Sarah looked out the

65

window and stiffened. Nathan followed her look. A shiny silver Lexus pulled into a parking spot. A smartly dressed woman in dress pants and a black wool coat got out and walked toward the front door of the restaurant. "—um, the animals we just learned about," finished Sarah. "Hey, that's my mom. I need to go."

Nathan got out of the booth, and Sarah's face made it clear he hadn't hurried fast enough.

"Bye," she called over her shoulder as she ran to the door.

She met her mother just as the woman entered the restaurant, but they didn't leave. Nathan's hands went sweaty. Sarah caught his gaze and raised her eyebrows. Her mother seemed to be asking a lot of questions, and Sarah seemed reluctant to answer. It's like they were a film running at two different speeds—her mother on fast-forward, and Sarah on slow motion.

Sarah and her mom placed an order at the cash register. Nathan rose and walked toward where they stood waiting for their food. Sarah's mother was saying, "Is Carly ever not fine?"

"Are you asking as a professional? Maybe she needs a chiropractic adjustment." There was a hint of exasperation in Sarah's voice.

"I'm quite busy enough," her mother replied.

As Nathan approached, Sarah gave him an almost imperceptible shake of her head. *Oh, great . . . she's embarrassed of me.* And here he'd thought she wanted to introduce him to her mother.

"Bye, Sarah," he said, changing his path and heading for the door.

"Bye," she said with a quick half-wave, then looked away.

Sarah's mother turned her sharp eyes on him. It wasn't necessarily a hostile look, but it was appraising. Nathan nodded at her. Sarah had acknowledged him, and now it was clear that her mother wanted to know how he fit into Sarah's life.

As he exited the restaurant, he thought, *Well, Mrs. Marshall, I'd like to understand that, too.*

11

Two Invitations

Mo sat cross-legged and leaned against her locker, then pulled a granola bar out of her lunch bag. Jessie had also brought lunch from home. Hannah had a yummy-smelling burger from the fundraiser.

Joe rounded the corner, and Mo's heart did that little flip it always did when she saw him, especially when she hadn't expected to. "Do you want to visit Sister Andrews with me this weekend?" he asked, dropping down beside Mo.

"Oh, she's the coolest. How is she?"

"Sister . . ." Jessie said. "I always think of nuns in long black dresses every time you guys talk like that."

"It's just how we address each other in the Church," Joe replied. "We're all part of God's family, so we call each other "Brother" and "Sister."

Jessie laughed. "I know, Maury's explained that before. But I still get a mental picture of a bunch of nuns." Jessie pressed her palms together as though she was praying.

Joe chuckled and then looked at Mo. "I told you Sister Andrews had a baby boy, right?"

"A nun having a baby?" Jessie giggled.

"She's a lady we did a service project for," Hannah said. "It was last June, I guess. Her husband died, and a bunch of the kids from our church laid the sod in her yard for her. Maury and Joe got to know her a little more than the rest of us. She wasn't feeling too well and you guys helped her, right?"

"Yeah, that's when she told us she was pregnant," Mo said. "I felt so bad for her, having a baby alone like that." There had been no father to help Bailey either, but it was because he didn't want to.

"Hmm. How awful to have your husband die," Jessie said, her flippant attitude gone. She lived with her dad and refused to discuss her family, so Mo had no idea what had happened to Jessie's mom.

Mo turned to Joe. "Yeah, I'd love to come with you. What's going on this weekend?"

"Well, I told you that my uncle is her . . ." He faltered over the next words. "Her . . . home teacher." Joe turned to Jessie. "That's another Church thing. We visit each other to talk about things like faith, and it's also so everyone has someone to call if they need help." After facing Mo again, Joe said, "He offered to paint the baby's room for her and was wondering if I'd like to help. I told him you might come along, too."

"Will Tyrone be there?" Hannah asked.

"Oh, Hannah, sorry—I should have made it clear. I was just inviting Mo. My uncle only wanted one or two more people."

"Oh," Hannah said, frowning a little. "Joe's cousin Tyrone is so good-looking." She turned to Mo. "Right, Maury?"

Joe's eyes were riveted on Mo. Glancing away from his penetrating gaze, she said, "Yeah, he's cute," then pulled out a bag of mini carrots and offered them to her friends.

Joe took one. "So, do you want to come?"

It could've been Mo's imagination, but he seemed less excited about the trip now. "I'll have to try to get someone to take my shift at work," she said, "but I'll try. I'll let you know."

That night, Mo was in the staff break room at McDonalds, poring over her Social Studies notes. She had a test in two days, and there was a lot to memorize. The chicken burger she'd eaten for dinner was sitting like a lump in her stomach. She took a sip of her orange soda, then repeated the words from her notes.

"Oh, very good. I'll give you an A-plus, Miss Matheson." It was Garrett. He looked over her shoulder. "I remember that stuff. Do you have Mr. Sam?"

"No, I have Mr. Ford."

"That's him. Sam Ford."

"Oh." Mo turned to face her coworker. "Hey, what are you doing this weekend? I noticed—"

"Are you asking me out?" Garrett grinned with his usual boyish charm.

Mo rolled her eyes. "No, I'm wondering if you'll work my shift on Saturday. I noticed you aren't on the schedule."

"I suppose I could work for you. But what's in it for me?"

Mo laughed. "They *will* pay you, you know."

"Yeah, but I'm doing you a favor, so what are you going to do for me?"

"I'll work for you sometime when you need a day off," she said.

Garrett gave her an annoyed smile. "Okay, I guess that's good enough."

"Look, if you don't want to, just say so. Megan isn't working either, so I can ask her." Mo went back to her notes but couldn't concentrate on the words, with Garrett standing there looking at her.

He came around the table and sat across from her. "I was just joking around. Actually, I was trying to say that it would be cool to go out sometime, but it came out wrong."

"Okay," Mo said, unable to hold back a smile.

"'Okay' you forgive me? Or 'okay' you'll go out with me?"

Mo shrugged. "Both."

"Wow, awesome," Garrett said, back to his teasing tone.

"I was supposed to work eleven to seven. I'll let Ken know you're taking that shift for me."

Garrett nodded. "All right. Do you want to see a show next week?"

"I don't know. We'll have to see when we both have a day off. Oh, and we'll have to invite some other people along. I only date in groups."

"You really don't trust me, do you?"

"Maybe not. But I only date in groups, even with guys I do trust."

"You're serious?"

"Yeah, totally."

Garrett huffed. "Does your family have a nanny that will be joining us?"

"Just a group of kids will be fine." When he didn't respond, Mo said, "Look, that's the way it is, Garrett. Do you still want to work for me on Saturday?"

He shook the bangs from his eyes and stifled a burp. "You have a lot of conditions, but okay."

She and Garrett were working in different areas that day. She was assembling orders during the busy times, and he was working the fryers again. During a slow patch, Mo went to wipe down tables. Garrett joined her with a cloth in his hand.

"So, just how many guys to do want me to bring along on this group date of ours? How many do you think you can handle? Eight? Ten?"

"Great idea, speed dating. We'll be out in public." Mo narrowed her eyes at him. "And I'll spend fifteen minutes talking to each of you and get to know a whole bunch of new guys all in one date."

Garrett gave her an innocent look. "What? You said I had to have a group. How many guys make a group?"

Mo wiped the next table, while Garrett skimmed the seats with his cloth as if he really didn't care if he got them clean or not.

"I'll give you the definition of a group," Mo said. "It is a collection of youth, all about the same age, but varying in personality, socioeconomic backgrounds, and gender. In other words, both boys and girls must be present."

"Sounds like you're a little bit too into Social Studies. Are you memorizing the textbook?"

"Studying is a good thing. You should try it sometime."

"So you don't want a bunch of guys all to yourself?"

Mo rolled her eyes again.

12

Undisclosed Trials

Mo got home from work that night smelling like cleaning solution and grease. The walk in the cold air had felt so nice.

"You didn't call for a ride," Nathan said from where he sat at the kitchen table, eating a big bowl of cereal.

"No. It's not that cold." Mo removed her thick mittens and winter coat. She headed toward her bedroom. As she passed Bailey's room, Bailey called, "Hey, Maury, come here."

Bailey sat on her bed holding a piece of paper. "Something's wrong. I've read the note again and again."

"Note?" Mo sat at the foot of the bed.

"It's certainly too short to call a letter." Bailey flipped the paper to reveal half a page of loopy handwriting with a lot of white space around the words. Mo took the page and read:

Dear Bailey,

I know you've probably been waiting for this letter. Sorry it has been so long in coming. Things are busy here and we have our trials. Life has a way of throwing difficulties your way when you least expect it.

Brooke laughs and is loving her tummy time. I think she's thinking about crawling. She is surprising us with her appetite. We have to keep asking her, "Do you want some more?" so often that she tries to say "more." Sorry, no pictures to send this time.

Love,
Laura

Mo looked up. "Yeah, it does sound like something might be wrong. What do you think it is?"

"Okay, so there was the cute little anecdote of Brooke wanting more helpings of dinner," Bailey said. "She's growing up—asking for the things she wants, exerting her will. It's kind of a milestone. Pretty soon she'll be a toddler, not a baby. But Laura talks about trials, so I'm worried."

"Yeah. But everyone has trials, Bailey."

"I know, but what if Brooke is sick? What if she has some awful disease that Laura didn't want to tell me about?"

Mo shook her head. "I doubt it. I really think she'd tell you if it was something serious."

"Hopefully, but maybe not. Or maybe it's money problems. Their finances were really tight before, and maybe they're worse now."

Mo grimaced. "It's a possibility."

"She shouldn't say 'We have our trials' if she's not going to explain what they are. I mean, maybe Tom or Laura is sick. People get cancer every day, even people like them, in their thirties. Or maybe they aren't getting along. That's it! I bet Laura and Tom are getting a divorce." Bailey grabbed a square throw pillow beside her and punched it. "I didn't give up my baby for adoption so she could end up living in two different homes, with Mom one week and with Dad the next."

"You're totally overreacting, Bailey. Trials could be anything."

"Exactly! What the heck is going on?"

Mo put her hand on Bailey's knee. "I'm sure she'll give you more details in her next letter. Just try not to worry."

"That's impossible."

"Yeah," Mo sighed.

13

Painting and Flirting

Joe drove up to Mo's house in a Pontiac Sunfire, the Parker family's second car. He got out and walked toward the front door. He wore tan cotton pants and a blue-and-white-striped golf shirt. He looked so tall, and his dark hair was damp and curly at the base of his neck.

Mo stepped away from the living room window. She was wearing gray cut-off sweats and a tie-dyed T-shirt that was frayed around the collar. Mo answered the door and pointed at Joe's nice clothes. "Are you going to paint in those?"

"I have painting clothes in the car. If we have time after, we could hit West Ed. What do you say?" The West Edmonton Mall was one of the biggest malls in the world.

"Sure. I'll be back in a second." Mo left him at the door and went to her room. She dumped her gym bag out on her bed and put her favorite jeans and a burgundy long sleeve casual top inside the bag. Then, as an afterthought, she threw in a lip gloss and eyeliner, too.

A minute later, she slipped into the bucket seat of the Sunfire. She had to force herself not to stare at Joe. Lately, he seemed cuter every time she saw him. As they left St. Paul, she said,

"Thanks for letting me grab some other clothes. I hadn't even thought about doing something after."

"Yeah, you're pretty focused. That's probably what makes you such a good basketball player—your focus, your intensity."

Mo shrugged. "And what's the secret to your success? Your basketball success, I mean."

Joe grinned sheepishly. "Raw talent?"

"Ha ha. Yes, of course."

"Growing a full three inches last summer didn't hurt any, either."

"We used to be about the same height," Mo commented.

Joe sat taller in the seat. "But not anymore, little girl."

The two-hour drive to Edmonton seemed to be over in no time as they talked and laughed. Their conversation came to a stop, however, as Joe maneuvered through the heavy city traffic.

"I thought Sister Andrew's house was on that side of the highway," Mo said, pointing.

"I'm going to my uncle's."

"Oh."

Joe seemed to relax when they left the main roads and entered a residential area. "We'll ride with them to Sister Andrew's place, which is good, because I don't remember exactly where she lives." Joe stopped in front of a white split-level house with dark-green trim. They got out of the car.

Tyrone flung open the screen door and hurried toward them. His hair was the same blond as the last time she'd seen him, but his shoulders seemed broader. His smile was the type you'd see on the cover of a teen magazine under the title "Where to Meet Great Guys."

"Hey," he called. His gaze locked on Mo as she approached him. "I thought you were going to start coming to more stake activities, Maury."

"I'm still planning on it."

"Hi," said Joe in a tone that made it clear he wasn't thrilled to see Tyrone.

Mr. Brand emerged from the open garage, carrying a box with paint trays and rollers sticking out of it. "Oh good, you made it." He placed the box in the trunk of a Honda Civic that was probably fifteen years old.

"You can ride shotgun," Tyrone told Joe.

Mo and Tyrone got in the back seat. Joe looked at his cousin through narrowed eyes but got in the front passenger seat. Mr. Brand was driving.

"Sister Andrews will be excited to see you two again," said Mr. Brand as they pulled away from the house. "She has mentioned you several times since we all laid the sod. You must have really hit it off."

"We did," Joe said. "She's a great lady."

"How is she doing? How's her baby?" asked Mo.

"Hardly a baby anymore. He's crawling around and getting into everything. It's hard on Sister Andrews to leave him with a babysitter every day. But what else can a single mother do?"

Mo had hated it when her mom started working again after her dad died, and Mo had been thirteen years old at the time.

"There's a stake dance next week," Tyrone told her. "Why don't you come?"

"Maybe I will."

Joe shifted in his seat, and the back of his neck turned red. Mo frowned. *I can't believe he would be upset about me going to a stake dance. If I find a ride, there will probably be room for him, too.*

The car stopped in front of Sister Andrew's big house. "That sure was a lot of grass," Mo mused.

Tyrone, Mo, Joe, and Mr. Brand strode up the walkway to the front door. Mr. Brand carried the box of supplies. Before Joe could ring the bell, the door flew open and a tired but happy-looking woman welcomed them into the house. She opened her arms wide and enveloped first Joe in a hug, and then Mo.

"How are you? You look great," Mo said. Somehow, Sister Andrews seemed less vulnerable now.

"I'm fine. You'll have to meet my son, but right now he's sleeping."

"We're ready to get to work," Mr. Brown said.

"I haven't seen these kids for so long," said Sister Andrews, "and they worked so hard last time they were here." She directed a fake scowl toward Mr. Brand. "You don't have to be such a slave driver, Lyle."

"I worked hard," said Tyrone. "But Joe was kind of wimpy, as I recall. Don't you still owe me a chocolate bar or something?"

Joe tried to smile, but it came off looking like he'd eaten a rotten tomato. "You'll get it."

"Grab the plastic," Brother Brand told his son.

"Want to help me?" Tyrone asked Mo. She followed him to the open trunk, and together they brought out a large piece of thick plastic folded several times over. The March wind tried to whip it from their grasp, and Mo almost lost the corner.

"I think this was the covering for some furniture we ordered. I started to throw it away, but Dad basically tackled me to stop me." Tyrone laughed. "He couldn't believe I would throw away . . . packaging!"

Mo noted the splatters of tan- and coral-colored paint on it as they carried it between them toward the house. "Looks like it's had some use."

Tyrone chuckled. "It's been very useful garbage."

With the plastic between them, they reached the open door. "We're too wide like this," Mo said.

"Unless we can kind of fold it in the middle," Tyrone said. They tried but it was too thick and didn't want to fold. "We need to turn."

Mo started to go in first, but so did Tyrone. "We're not in sync," she said. They shared a smile.

"You go first," he said.

As they crossed the threshold, Sister Andrews led the way down the hall and said, "It's this room."

Mo and Tyrone unfolded the plastic and spread it out. The huge sheets of plastic covered most of the carpet but didn't line up at the corners. When Tyrone pulled one way, Mo's side came away, and when she lined her side up, his came away. "Work with me, here," she said, laughing.

From the doorway, Joe said, "It doesn't have to be perfect." He had changed into a gray shirt that must have been washed a thousand times. "The plastic can curl up at the wall a bit." He gave a little jerk to Tyrone's side of the plastic and it shifted to cover the carpet and the baseboard on his side.

Tyrone laughed. "How did you do that?"

"It's not rocket science," Joe said in a grumpy tone. He left and returned with a can of paint.

Mr. Brand brought in the rollers and paint trays. Mo and Tyrone shared a tray on one side of the room, and Mr. Brand and Joe used the other one.

At one point, Joe came up behind them and said, "There's a spot dripping right there, Tyrone." Joe reached around him and rolled the paint roller over the drip.

A few minutes later, Joe returned and told Tyrone, "You got some on the trim. You need to be more careful."

Is it Joe's life-long goal to be a precision house painter? Or does he just enjoy pointing out Tyrone's mistakes?

Sister Andrews helped them with the painting until the soft cry of a baby drew her away. Then she appeared in the doorway with her infant son. He had huge dark-brown eyes. "He's adorable," Mo said as she set her roller back in the tray.

"This is Kenny," said Sister Andrews. "He has his father's eyes." A flicker of sadness passed over her face.

This little boy would never know his father. A wave of emotion swept over Mo, and tears came to her eyes before she could check them. In that moment, looking at a little boy who would never know his father, Mo missed her dad fiercely. The ache never completely left her chest. Even when she was laughing with her friends or studying for a test, the pain was still there, lying dormant like a lion ready to pounce.

"Could you help me with Kenny for a few minutes?" Sister Andrews asked.

Grateful for the escape, Mo followed her out of the room. "I'm sorry," said Mo when they reached the kitchen. "I don't know what's the matter with me."

Sister Andrews motioned toward a kitchen chair, and Mo sat. "I do," said Sister Andrews. "Lyle told me your dad passed away. I'm so, so sorry." Tears streamed down Mo's face as Sister Andrews placed her baby in a mechanical swing that stood between the kitchen and living room. She started the swinging and the baby quieted.

Sister Andrews set a box of tissue on the table and took the chair next to Mo. Mo wiped her eyes, and then it all tumbled out. She told Sister Andrews about the fire and how her father appeared to be getting better. "Then he came to the school for our basketball tournament," Mo continued. "Dad was my coach." She paused, remembering all the time they spent together with basketball. "He started to feel lousy, so we rushed him back to the hospital. He had an infection, and his lungs were very damaged." Mo's voice caught on the last word. She swallowed hard. "The worst part of it all is that he could have been okay." Her words were strong and bitter now. "The rest of us recovered from the smoke inhalation, but Dad was in the house so much longer. It could have been avoided. If he got out sooner . . . If he hadn't breathed in so much smoke . . ."

Sister Andrews grabbed a tissue. Her eyes were spilling over with tears. "The 'what ifs' can drive you mad."

"When you said Kenny has his father's eyes, I just felt so bad knowing what he was missing and what I'm missing—"

"Gary had cancer," Sister Andrews said softly. "It started in his stomach, but it metastasized, and pretty soon it was everywhere. It was all so sudden, and even though it was several months before he died, it seems like one day he was fine, the next he had stomach pain, and the next he was gone."

"I'm not sure going fast is good for those of us left behind," Mo said.

"Exactly! How can someone who is such a huge part of your life be gone so suddenly?"

"My dad really meant a lot to me, but a husband? He'd mean everything."

Sister Andrews pressed her lips into a hard line and nodded. "It's been devastating. Brother Brand has helped a lot through this time." She took a deep breath. "And it's starting to get better. But you have comfort I don't have, remember?" Sister Andrews passed the box of Kleenex to Mo after taking another tissue herself. "You're sealed to your family."

"Couldn't you go to the temple now, even though he's—"

"I could." Sister Andrews wiped her eyes again. "But Gary was against the Church when he died, so I don't think he would want the work done for him. Maybe someday I'll feel it's the right thing to do, but not now."

Joe, Tyrone, and Mr. Brand finished painting the baby's room and started on the playroom. "I should go help them," Mo said finally.

"We're going to be okay," Sister Andrews said firmly as she and Mo rose from the table.

Mo nodded.

"You can call me Carol," said Sister Andrews. "We've cried together. We're friends."

Mo smiled. "You can call me Maury. All my friends do." She stuttered slightly as she remembered Joe. "Except Joe," she admitted in a small voice. "He calls me Mo, and you can too if you'd like."

"I'll stick with Maury."

"Okay." Even though Joe was acting like the painting police today, she liked him more than she often let on, even to Hannah and Jessie.

So, whether it was admiration or esteem or even the big L word that she felt for Joe, he was her first date. She was just at the edge, looking into the dating scene.

Kenny, the baby, awoke in his swing. "Well, I can't put him off any longer," said his mother. "I have to feed him now."

Mo joined the painters in the second room. Tyrone smiled at her. "Oh, so you have decided to join us," he said. "First Joe was slacking when we laid sod, and now you are slacking off painting." Tyrone shook his head. "He's been a bad influence on you. You need to hang around someone more responsible. Someone like . . . oh, I don't know, me." Tyrone's smile was infectious.

"You're making a puddle on the drop cloth," Joe snapped.

Tyrone looked down. His roller was dripping between his feet. "Oops." He stopped to mop up the paint with a rag, then whispered to Mo, "See what you do to me."

Before long the room was finished, the rollers and brushes were clean, and everything was packed up in Brother Brand's box.

"What do you like on a pizza?" asked Carol Andrews, holding a cell phone in one hand and a take-out menu in the other.

"No, no," protested Brother Brand. "You don't have to feed us."

"These two have a couple-hour drive ahead of them." Carol pointed to Joe and Mo.

"Don't worry. I won't send them away hungry."

"Okay," Carol said. "Don't wait so long before you visit again. And you don't always have to do work here."

Mo chuckled. "Oh, Carol, we don't mind."

Joe raised his eyebrows. "Carol?"

"It's still Sister Andrews to you," Sister Andrews teased.

"That's right," Mo said. "Until you've cried together, you can't reach our level of friendship."

"I was full-fledged blubbering," Carol said. "We're blubber buddies."

"Blubber buddies forever," Mo repeated as Carol Andrews hugged her tight.

14

West Ed Tension

Joe drove up and down the aisles of cars at the West Edmonton Mall. Finally, he found a space and carefully parked the Sunfire. "I can't believe he's coming with us," he muttered.

"Hmm," Mo said, and got out of the car.

She and Joe were walking toward the entrance when Tyrone's voice rang out behind them. "Joe. Maury." She turned and he sprinted up to them. "We had to park in the last rows," he complained. "It's always crazy here on the weekends."

The mall was huge. It was like entering a town under a single roof. They walked by the skating rink. "That's an Olympic-size rink," Tyrone said.

"Wow," Mo said. "Hey, before we eat, let's see what time the next dolphin show starts. I haven't been here since I was little, but I was so excited about the dolphins!"

"Sounds like you still are," Tyrone said. "You liked it better than the amusement park?"

"Oh yeah. I forgot there was an amusement park inside here, too."

"Everyone knows about the amusement park," Joe whispered.

"Have you been to the wave pool?" asked Tyrone.

Mo shook her head. "No. Can we see it from the mall?"

"Sure. There are big windows."

Joe fell a step behind. When Mo met his eyes, he had an ornery look on his face.

"The next dolphin show is in half an hour," Mo said, pointing to the sign.

"We don't really have time to go anywhere to eat," Tyrone said, "unless you want to pay for seats close to the tank. If we want to find standing room, we better save our spots now."

"Why would we pay for seats?" Mo asked. "You can see perfectly from here."

"That's what I think," said Tyrone. "How about if Joe saves us space and we run and get something to eat?"

"That sounds like a great idea." Joe's voice was full of sarcasm.

"We'll get something for you," said Tyrone. Brother Brand had given Tyrone some money for the three of them to have dinner. "What do you want? A hamburger? A wrap?"

"Surprise me," Joe said.

"Here, take my jacket," Mo told him. "Put it over the rail to save my spot."

"I'm not taking my hoodie off," Tyrone said. "Just try to look wide."

Mo giggled, and she and Tyrone hurried away. The line was shortest at Dairy Queen, so they went there and ordered hamburgers and milkshakes.

It was almost time for the show to begin by the time they returned. As Joe took Mo's coat off the railing, he muttered, "Finally."

"We hurried as fast as we could," Mo replied.

"Well, while you guys were running about the mall I was repeating, 'I'm saving this spot for friends,' about fifteen times."

After the show began, Mo said, "They are so sleek. So beautiful." She held her breath when a dolphin sprang from the water to touch its nose on a bright-orange ball. When the show ended, Mo clapped louder than Tyrone and Joe put together.

"Sometimes we come to the mall just to watch them," Tyrone said. "I wander around between their shows and come back two or three times. But now, how about the amusement park?"

"Sure," said Mo.

"Why not?" Joe said.

Tyrone was a chatty tour guide. Mo chuckled at his stories, but Joe exhaled sharply a couple of times. "We can't stay long," Joe said as they approached Galaxyland.

"Do you want to go on any rides?" Tyrone asked Mo.

"Maybe just a couple. What do you think, Joe?"

"Yeah." He was a little bit more enthusiastic now.

"I love the pirate-ship ride," Mo said.

They bought tickets and got in line.

"It's so loud in here," complained Joe as the roller coaster roared above their heads.

When it was their turn to board, the ship was almost full. "It's best at the back," Tyrone said. He sat at the far end and pointed for Mo to sit next to him. There was a single spot in the seat in front of him, too.

She slipped in beside Tyrone, while Joe sat in front.

"I'll try not to get sick in your hair, Cuz," Tyrone said.

Joe didn't turn around or respond.

The ship started to sway forward and back, gaining height with each swing. Mo and Tyrone lifted their hands in the air. "Whoa!" she yelled as she lifted in her seat. Of course, the bar across her lap held down her thighs.

"How about the bumper cars next?" Mo asked as they exited the ride.

"That's a great idea," Joe said with a glint in his eye.

After Mo buckled herself into the bumper car, she grabbed the wheel and waited for power. "You boys are in trouble," she called. Tyrone took a car next to her, and Joe took one on the other side of Tyrone. She hit Tyrone at the same time as Joe did. Then she backed up. Joe's car seemed stalled. It stopped completely for several seconds. That made him an easy target, and Tyrone gave him a hard, head-on smash.

Afterwards, Mo said, "One more ride. The swings."

"No way," said Tyrone.

"I don't trust that ride," Joe said.

"Oh, come on. Look, there are little kids on it," said Mo. "If they can handle it, you guys can."

"Fine," said Tyrone. Then he proceeded to scream throughout the entire ride.

Joe was laughing hard from his vantage place on solid ground.

Finally, the swings lowered and Tyrone and Mo exited. "That was insanity," said Tyrone.

"I've never heard you scream like that," Joe called as he met them.

Tyrone laughed. "And you'll never hear it again. That was terrifying."

"I was laughing at you so hard I couldn't really enjoy the ride," Mo said. "Let's go again."

Tyrone put an arm around her shoulder. "You will never get me on that ride again."

"We better leave," Joe suggested. "Winter driving at night can get sketchy."

"Just a little longer," Tyrone replied.

"No. It's not a good idea." Joe's tone was firm.

"I could hold you here captive if I wanted," Tyrone said. "I'm sure you'd never be able to find your car without my help."

"That's probably true. Do we go in that direction?" Mo pointed. "I'm so confused here."

"We came in by The Bay," Joe said calmly.

"And which way is that?" Tyrone asked.

"I don't know, but I can read a mall map if you won't tell us."

Tyrone laughed and Mo joined him. "He's just kidding," she said.

As they walked through what seemed like miles of hallways and endless clothing stores, Joe fell a step behind again.

Out in the parking lot, the wind had picked up, and Mo's hair was whipping her face. She stopped to wait for Joe to join them as she had done several times in the mall. Her hair was flipping into her eyes and she was laughing in her frustration to see. She met Joe's eyes. He smiled back at her, and for a moment there was just the two of them in the middle of the crowded city.

He reached for her hand, but she let go a second later to tame her hair again. Then there was Tyrone, his hand above her elbow. He said, "Thanks for helping with the painting today. And don't forget what I said about the next stake dance. Come if you can."

"Okay," Mo said.

The ride back to St. Paul in the dark would have been in almost complete silence if it hadn't been for the radio. Mo tried to start a conversation, first about Sister Andrews, and then about the size of the West Edmonton Mall, but Joe hardly spoke in return. Eventually, Mo stopped trying. Joe had acted strange all day. His threat to seek out a mall map if Tyrone wouldn't show them the way to their car was the strangest of all.

"What are you thinking about?" Joe asked suddenly.

"Tyrone," she replied.

Joe swallowed audibly. "You two seemed to really hit it off today."

"We did," Mo said simply.

There was a stretch of over a minute. The radio news was on. It was seven o'clock. "He is a nice guy," Joe admitted.

"Am I allowed to talk to other guys, Joe?"

"What's that supposed to mean?"

"It means you're acting strange. You're acting mad at me."

"I'm not mad at you."

"Pouty, then."

"Well, I was kind of hoping that we'd have a nice day together, but you just wanted to flirt with Tyrone. Glad I could give you a ride."

Mo's face flushed with anger. "Yeah, thanks for the ride," she snapped.

The last few miles to town stretched out before them. Joe turned up the radio. The nothingness of the songs and chatter filled the emptiness of the little car. Instead of being a distraction for Mo's anger, though, it intensified it.

When Joe pulled up in front of Mo's house, she got out and slammed the door before he could put the car in park.

15

Goals of Neon Bowling

"We've got a bus!" yelled the A&W manager.

Nathan filled the fry baskets and lowered them into the bubbling oil. Sarah had a line of teen burgers that were partly finished. She shook her head and started two more. Nathan came to her side. "Did you lose count?"

"Just panicking a bit," she said. "Guess I'll keep making them until somebody tells me to stop."

He helped at her station until the buzz of the timers took him back to the fryers. He filled the fry boxes, then returned to help Sarah catch up while he waited for a batch of onion rings. "Thanks," she said as she slipped the last burger into a slot in the metal warming tray.

"No problem. What's a boyfriend for?" The words slipped out before Nathan could stop them. Sarah's eyes went wide, and Nathan's face turned hot in an instant. He started to turn away, but she caught his arm and stared at him.

"There's neon bowling after eleven tonight," he said.

Sarah smiled. "Sounds great."

Once the store was closed, they rushed through cleanup and went to change. A few minutes later, Nathan was waiting in the hallway when Sarah's voice rang out from the girl's locker room. "I'm going neon bowling with Nathan." There was a pause. "Well, he must not think I'm *that* crazy." Another pause. "I gotta go. We'll talk later." She walked out of the locker room and put her cell phone in her bag.

"Did you tell your parents you'll be home later than usual?" Nathan asked.

"No. I guess I should call them."

Soon she was speaking into the phone. "Hi, Mom. I'm going neon bowling so I'll be home late." There was a brief pause, and then she said. "Someone from work. Okay, bye."

As they walked through the mostly deserted parking lot, Sarah shivered. *If I was really her boyfriend, I would put my arm around her,* Nathan thought. He helped her into the passenger side of the car, then hurried around to start the engine and get the heater going.

"Thanks," Sarah said, smiling.

Soon they were lacing up their bowling shoes and laughing at how their teeth glowed in the neon light.

"You go first," Sarah said.

Nathan chose a ball, lined up his shot, and let the ball go. Several pins toppled over, and with the next ball, he got the spare.

Sarah didn't knock down a single pin on her turn. It turned out that Sarah was the worst bowler Nathan had ever seen, and that included the little kids two lanes over who spread their legs and launched the ball like a water balloon. Sarah used a more mature stance, but he almost suggested she try the child version. The little kids, undoubtedly up later than their bedtimes, were hitting more pins than Sarah.

She hardly seemed to notice her terrible score, though. She smiled and returned to the bench with a skip in her step after throwing consecutive gutter balls. Maybe she was doing it on purpose. Even beginner bowlers hit a few pins now and then, simply by luck. Sarah hit a grand total of three pins the first game.

After one of her balls scampered down the gutter, Sarah said, "You know it's really not so hard to keep the ball away from those pins. Why are you having so much trouble with it, Nathan?"

"The idea is to knock them down," he began until he was stopped short by the grin on her face.

"It's so messy the way you bowl," she said. "The machine has to pick up after you over and over again."

"I suppose I should pick up after myself." For the rest of the game, it was Nathan's challenge to come as close to the pins as he could without actually knocking any down.

"Now you're getting the hang of it," Sarah told him.

They laughed together most of the evening, and Nathan had such a great time, he almost forgot about the fire.

When Sarah happened to knock down two pins together, she feigned a disappointed look and came over to Nathan, saying, "Oh, no, I blew it!" He put his arms around her and patted her back. "It's okay. Better luck next time."

She looked up into his face, and his eyes met hers. In the dim light of neon bowling, she was irresistible. He lowered his head and kissed her. When they parted Nathan whispered, "I've been your boyfriend all this time and never kissed you until now."

"It's about time," Sarah said.

"I better get you home."

"We still have two frames to go."

"Well, let's just throw the ball down there, and who cares how well we do."

The next frame, Nathan got two strikes and Sarah hit three pins, then got a spare in the tenth frame. She couldn't have looked more surprised.

"What a mess you've made!" Nathan teased.

Nathan returned their shoes. When he turned around, Sarah was talking to a tall, muscular guy who had to be a football player. He sat pretty close to her, and Sarah spoke with animation when she answered him. Nathan had seen the young man at school. He was in Sarah's grade—and he was the kind of guy the girls drooled over. And Nathan wasn't. He hung back and put on his outdoor shoes. Then, when he had nothing else to do, he started toward Sarah. The guy said goodbye and walked away just before Nathan approached. He sat down and handed over her shoes. "That guy wasn't bothering you, was he?" he asked, even though it was obviously not what was happening.

Sarah shook her head.

After they were buckled into his car, Nathan asked, "So, just for the record, how long have we been dating."

"I'd have to look in my diary," said Sarah with a smirk.

He started the car and pulled out of the parking lot. "I don't want to miss an anniversary or anything."

"You're so sweet."

He chuckled.

"What do you think of lying?" asked Sarah.

Nathan laughed. "You saying I'm not sweet?"

"No. You are. But just in general."

He turned onto her street. "Lying?" Scriptures came to his mind about bearing false witness, but he took a lighter approach. "I'm against it," he said.

"Against it?"

"Yes. I'm anti-lying. Pro truth-telling. Why? Are you going to tell me that this is really our first date? I haven't been your boyfriend for a long, though undisclosed, time?"

Sarah's laugh seemed forced.

He parked at the curb in front of her house.

"I think my parents would like to meet you," said Sarah.

Nathan looked at his watch. "Will they be up?"

She nodded.

"Okay," he said, then got out of the car and opened Sarah's door.

The front door of the house flung open just as they reached the top step. A tall man stood imposingly in the frame. Surprised,

Nathan stepped back and had to grab the railing to keep from falling. Sarah gave him a meek smile. They slipped off their shoes in the entranceway and followed her father into the living room.

"This is Nathan Matheson, my date tonight," Sarah explained.

Her father's lips became a straight line as he nodded and made a noise in the back of his throat. "He graduated last year and works with me," Sarah continued.

"You finished high school last year, and you still work at A&W," Mr. Matheson said. "Is this a career choice, or don't you have any ambition?"

Nathan's mouth went suddenly dry. Mr. Marshall pointed at the couch, and it seemed more an order than an invitation. Nathan sat and Sarah followed. "I actually have two jobs right now," Nathan said. "Besides A&W, I work at the steel company, but neither is my ultimate goal. I especially don't want to work the closing shift at a fast-food restaurant for the rest of my life.

"What is your ultimate goal?" Mr. Marshall asked.

"I—I haven't decided."

"Are you going to go to university?" said a higher-pitched voice behind Nathan. He jumped. Mrs. Marshall must have walked into the room with the stealth of a cat. She perched on the love seat next to her husband.

Sarah placed her hand on Nathan's knee as though to calm him, but it only made him more nervous, especially with the heat of her hand coming through his jeans. Her parents were staring him down like they knew he had kissed Sarah earlier that night. You don't touch someone's knee if you haven't already kissed them. Nathan had no idea what he'd been thinking, kissing her on their first date.

"Or college, at least," Mr. Marshall was saying.

"Uh, yes, someday, yes," Nathan replied.

"When might that day be?" Mr. Marshall asked. "Five years, ten, twenty?"

"Well, right after my mission."

"Mission?" Mrs. Marshall whispered something under her breath with a tart laugh.

"Yes. It's a church mission," Nathan said.

At this, Sarah's parents huffed in exasperation. Mrs. Marshall might have even rolled her eyes. "When will this mission happen?" Mr. Marshall said, continuing the interrogation.

"I'll probably be leaving in August."

Mrs. Marshall nodded. "Are you building houses in Africa or something?"

"No," said Nathan. He said a quick silent prayer. "I will give some service, but mostly I'll be preaching the gospel of Jesus Christ."

Mr. Marshall swore under his breath. "How much time are you wasting with this pursuit?"

Drops of sweat sprang up on the back of Nathan's neck. "I don't consider it a waste, sir, but I'll be gone for two years."

"Two years?" Mrs. Marshall sounded angry now. "And this seems rational to you?" She glared at Sarah.

"It's more than rational, Mrs. Marshall. It's my duty to God."

"It's been very interesting meeting you," Mr. Marshall said. He and his wife stood. "I'm rather glad, however, that you will soon be gone preaching and not dating our daughter." With that, Sarah's parents left the room.

Nathan felt like he'd been holding his breath. This was rougher than any job interview he'd ever had.

"Sorry," Sarah said.

"Uh, it's okay."

The phone rang. Sarah went to the table beside the couch and lifted the receiver. Her father's voice blared through the phone, "Do you have any idea what time it is?"

A soft female voice replied, "Sorry. I just wanted to ask Sarah about her date."

"I have it, Dad," said Sarah, glancing at Nathan. She waited until her father hung up then said, "Hi, Lindsey. Is Carly there?"

After a beat, Sarah said, "Hi, Carly. I'll call you back in just a minute. I know. It would be great if I had more minutes on my cell phone. We say that every day . . . yes, just leaving."

Sarah's friend said, "He kissed you." It wasn't a question. *She must have been at the bowling alley,* Nathan thought. Sarah hung up without responding.

Sarah linked her arm in Nathan's as they walked to the front door. "I should have warned you how they are about religion. I didn't realize it would come up right away." There was a pained look on her face.

Nathan only nodded.

Sarah released his arm. "Good-night, Nathan."

He mumbled a good-night, tried to smile at her, and made his way to his car.

16

A Gift for Sarah

"I really want to go to the stake dance," Maury said a few days later as everyone helped Mom prepare dinner.

Nathan measured the rice and water and set the pot on the stove. He stirred it once with a fork and turned the dial to bring it to a boil. He'd have to cook on his mission, so this was good practice. Stake dances had been few and far between for him. Living two hours from Edmonton and with no other kids his age in the branch, he rarely even thought about going.

Maury peeled the broccoli stalks and cut the flowerets into bite-size pieces.

"I love stir fry," Jordy said as he opened a can of baby corn.

Bailey looked up from chopping carrots. "I want to go in to Edmonton, too."

Mom met Bailey's eyes. "You want to go to the dance? I think that would be good for you—to hang out with other LDS kids. Meet some boys with good values."

"I don't want to go to the dance," Bailey corrected. "It's mostly younger kids there. While Maury goes to the dance, I can go see Brooke."

Mom's face fell and she exhaled loudly. "Brooke will be in bed by the time you get there if they are any kind of parents at all."

"That's exactly what I want to find out," Bailey said. "I leave messages on their answering machine, but they never call me back. She hasn't told me what trials they're having."

"Maybe it's personal," Nathan commented.

"She's the one who mentioned it—she brought it up. Then, I get nothing from her."

"Everybody has challenges, Bailey." Mom slammed the wok onto a burner. "The Andersons won't appreciate you barging into their home uninvited like someone from Child and Family Services who thinks they're hurting their child."

"*My* child."

Mom's face softened. "You need to move on, honey."

"I can't forget Brooke."

"I'm not saying you should, but—"

"Can I take the car to Edmonton or not?" Bailey interrupted.

Mom stared at her for a long moment. "I guess so. Maureen needs a ride. But to go see Laura and Tom . . . "

"I have every right to know what is going on with them if it affects my child."

Mom let out a sigh. "You are setting yourself up for heartache, Bailey."

"Well, it's my heart."

Nathan nibbled on a piece of carrot. *Maybe I'm setting myself up for heartache, too.* Sarah's parents thought he was a religious fanatic. Nathan had to talk to her about his beliefs, and he prayed she would be touched by the Spirit.

After dinner, Nathan played a couple of card games with Jordy, then put on his shoes and grabbed his car keys off the bench by the door.

"Where are you going?" asked Mom.

"I need to talk to Sarah. I won't be too late."

Mom lifted an eyebrow. "Okay."

Before he left, Nathan got a missionary copy of the Book of Mormon from his bedroom. He wrote a note to Sarah on the inside cover and signed his name. When he got in his car, he slipped the book into the glove compartment. He drove by Sarah's house twice before pulling to a stop at the curb.

He got out of the car and walked to the front door. He rang the bell and waited. *I should have called first.*

The porch light came on. Nathan could have sworn it was an 800-watt bulb, or whatever kind they used to light up the night sky outside a prison. Mr. Marshall opened the door. "Yes?"

"Is Sarah home?" Nathan mumbled.

"Nathan! Hi," Sarah said, appearing behind her dad. She slipped on a pair of shoes and grabbed a jacket from the closet. "Bye, Dad," she called as she exited the house.

Nathan stared and followed her.

"What?" she said, turning to him.

"Did you know I was coming over?"

She chuckled. "No. But I didn't want it to look like you drop by and expect me to be available. My mom, especially, wouldn't approve of that."

"It won't happen again."

"It can happen again and again. Just say 'I'm here to pick up Sarah.' Don't ask if I'm home."

"Okay, gotcha. But what if you're not home?" Nathan opened the car door and waited for her to get in.

Sarah laughed. "Well, then I guess we won't be going on a date that night."

A minute later, as he started the car and pulled away from the house, she said, "You're a brave guy, Nathan, coming back so soon after the ambush the other night." She made finger quotations around the word "ambush."

"Is it okay if we just go somewhere to talk?"

"About that?" Sarah said.

"About . . . everything." He drove to a park by the high school and stopped at the curb near the playground equipment. They got out and he held her hand as they walked toward the swings. A breeze teased her hair, and she smoothed it down with one hand.

"So, about my mission," Nathan began. "You know I'm a Christian, and you must know how important that is to me — important enough to spend two years of my life teaching others about it."

"I don't feel the way my parents do," Sarah said softly.

"Yeah, you obviously don't think I'm crazy like they do. But are you interested in religion? I mean, I care about you, and I want you to know what I know."

"This is your thing, Nathan. I admire you for it, but it's not my thing."

They reached the swings, which were swaying in the breeze. She let go of his hand and sank into one of the swings. He sat in the one next to her. "How can it not be your thing? If something is true, something that affects everything about life, then isn't it for everyone?"

With her feet on the ground, she swayed forward and back. "I suppose."

"Don't you believe in God?" Nathan said.

Sarah met his eyes and shrugged. "I don't know."

"What about Jesus? What do you know about him?"

"He taught people to be kind. And he was born at Christmas."

Nathan launched into a discussion about the role of Jesus as our Savior. Sarah asked some questions, but she seemed guarded as she listened to his answers. One topic led into others, and soon Nathan spoke of the pre-mortal world and the war in heaven, and baptism and temples.

Nathan had been so energized talking about the gospel that he hadn't noticed the passing of time until it was completely dark outside. "It must be getting late," he said.

"It *is* late," Sarah corrected.

"Sorry. I should take you home."

"I suppose," she said as she stood. "I want to understand you better."

They walked to the vehicle, and Nathan drove to her house. "I brought something for you," he said as the car rolled to a stop. He reached over and opened the glove compartment. "The Book of Mormon."

Sarah carefully removed the book, as though she was afraid it might bite her. "Nathan . . . uh, thank you. But I can't walk into the house with this in my hands. Mom and Dad would freak. And I'm not really interested in the nitty-gritty. But if you want to give it to me . . ." She looked in the back seat and reached over and grabbed a binder. "From high school?"

"I guess I should clean out my car."

She slipped the Book of Mormon between the pages of the binder. "Okay if I take this?"

"Sure," Nathan said.

He walked her to the door. "I'm glad you came by tonight," she said, holding the binder to her chest.

"Me too."

"Good-night." Sarah turned and was gone.

She had only taken the book to make him happy. She probably wouldn't even crack the cover. As Nathan drove home, he said a prayer—a prayer for Sarah Marshall.

17

The Dance Password

Mo and Bailey were in the front seat, with Hannah and Jessie in the back, when they drove to Edmonton for the dance that weekend. "So, it's at our stake center, right?" Bailey said to Mo.

"Yes. And I brought the map Nathan made after looking it up online."

"Steak center?" Jessie repeated. "It's being held at a restaurant?"

Mo looked back at Hannah, who smirked and said, "Yeah, so I hope you're hungry."

"Hungry enough for steak, and there might be a baked potato around," Mo said. "It *is* a steak center, and steak and potatoes go together."

"You didn't tell me this before," Jessie said. "Is there a dance floor off to the side or something?"

Mo shook her head. "No. We just dance around the tables."

"That sounds awkward," Jessie said.

"Oh no. That's how we always do it." Hannah giggled.

"That's too weird," Jessie replied. "Why is it really called a steak center?"

Mo explained that just like a local congregation is a branch or ward, a stake is a group of wards in an area.

"But you do know 'The Lord's Prayer,' don't you?" asked Hannah.

"Mostly." Now a crease formed in Jessie's forehead.

"Maybe you better practice it," Hannah said. "You have to say it to get into the dance."

"Like a password?"

Bailey gave Mo a look but then focused on her driving again.

"Kind of," Mo said. "They want to know you're, um, not going to come in and make trouble."

When Bailey pulled into the parking lot at the stake center, Mo and her friends spilled out.

Jessie scowled. "You guys are just trying to get me to make a fool of myself."

"No, I'm serious," Hannah insisted. "This is a church dance. If you don't do it right, they won't let you in. At least practice it one time."

"In my old school, we used to stand for the prayer every day, so I know it."

"Okay then. Walk right up to the table, recite the prayer, give them your dance card, and stick out your hand for a stamp." Hannah sounded very official.

"Your priest didn't say anything about that," said Jessie.

"Priest? Oh, you mean President Harris."

"Yeah. Before he gave me the dance card, he asked if I would follow the rules and not drink and stuff."

"Yeah, well this is one of the rules," Mo put in.

Hannah put a hand over her mouth to cover a giggle.

Jessie walked up to the table where the stake Young Women presidency was sitting and began, "'The Lord is my shepherd, I shall not want. He maketh me to lie down in green pastures' . . . Oh! That's the wrong one!"

Mo and Hannah exploded with laughter.

"Will you still let me in?" Jessie asked the Young Women leaders. "I know 'The Lord's Prayer.'"

Mo was laughing so hard, she had to rest her hands on her knees.

"They will if you have a dance card," said a familiar male voice.

Mo turned. Joe and his brother Mark were standing about six feet behind the girls.

"All you need is the card," Mark continued.

Jessie turned to Mo and Hannah. "I'm going to kill you guys!"

Hannah and Mo ran out the front door, with Jessie right behind them. She chased them over the grass and around the trees. She caught Hannah first and tackled her to the ground.

"I'm going to get grass stains on my shirt!" yelled Hannah.

Jessie knelt over her and pinned down her arms.

"Sorry, I'm sorry!" Hannah said, giggling. "You always say Mormons are kind of weird. I couldn't help myself."

Jessie grabbed a clump of brown grass, pulled it out of the ground, and rubbed it through Hannah's red hair before she let her up. "This was your idea," Jessie said to Mo, who was standing a few yards away. "Wasn't it?"

"Nuh-uh," said Mo.

"Right," Jessie said sarcastically. She ran after Mo, who darted around parked cars and trees. Jessie was panting, but Mo could have run much longer.

"Truce?" Mo said when Jessie was gasping for breath as she leaned against a pole. "If it makes you feel any better," Mo continued, "I'm sweating like crazy and I'm sure no one will want to dance with me now."

"Yes, you reek," laughed Jessie. "Okay, truce. I can't believe you guys messed with me so bad."

Mo laughed. "I can't believe you bought it. I really thought you figured out we were kidding. It will be like a school dance only with a little more light, and no music with bad lyrics."

Jessie laughed. "I can't believe I got nervous and quoted the only other Bible verse I know."

Mo stuck out her hand. "You're a great sport." The two girls shook hands and joined Hannah.

"She gets a handshake and I'm still shaking grass out of my hair!"

"Poor baby," Jessie teased.

With their dance cards in their hands, the three friends approached the table by the gym door. "Just a minute, girls," said one of the ladies. "Jessie's free to go in, but you two have to recite the Articles of Faith before you can enter the dance."

"What?" Mo gave an incredulous laugh.

"You heard me. Start at number one."

"All of them?" Hannah said.

"All thirteen Articles of Faith, word for word."

Joe appeared next to Jessie and asked, "Would you like to dance?"

"Sure." She gave Hannah and Mo a smug look.

Two of the Young Women leaders took Mo and Hannah aside, and they began at Article of Faith 1. Tyrone peeked out of the gym a few times, and the sight of him only made Mo more nervous, which meant she made more mistakes reciting the Articles of Faith. "Practice those for next time, girls," said one of the leaders when Hannah and Mo finally finished. "You never know when there might be a password or two or thirteen." Mo and Hannah laughed along with them as they returned to the table by the gym door. Then the two friends finally joined the other youth in the gym.

Tyrone was quickly at Mo's side. "Would you like to dance?"

"Sure."

He led her over to Jessie, who was dancing with Tyrone's friend. Mo recognized him from the activity last year at Sister Andrews' house. "Did you pass the test?" Jessie asked.

"Barely," Mo admitted.

The gym was full of people, and the girls hardly sat down. Mo danced with Tyrone several times, but not a single dance with Joe. Since their trip to Edmonton, they hadn't spoken much. Tonight Joe didn't seem pouty, simply busy dancing with other girls. About halfway through the evening, Mo looked over the shoulder of the guy she was dancing with and found Joe. The girl with him was laughing. They talked back and forth and seemed to be having a fun conversation.

Mo missed him. It had been weeks since that day at the West Edmonton Mall. It wasn't like they were mean to each other—they just stayed out of each other's way. They only had one class together, but they used to meet for a quick chat in the hallway and at lunch. Then, of course, there had been the rides home after school and the group dates.

When Joe wasn't acting jealous and possessive, Mo liked him a lot. But the snappy, grouchy guy she had ridden home from Edmonton with the other day wasn't someone she wanted to hang out with.

As the song ended, Mo thanked her partner and started off the dance floor. Tyrone met her. The dim light danced over his blond hair. He was kind of gorgeous, not to mention fun and upbeat.

The deejay announced the last song, and Mo accepted Tyrone's hand. They were holding hands on the way out to the dance floor! It was a dreamy slow song that Mo loved, and now it would always remind her of Tyrone Brand.

Bailey was nowhere in sight when Jessie, Hannah, and Mo left the building. They stood in a group, waiting. Joe walked by and said, "Did you girls enjoy the dance?" His gaze rested on Mo.

"It was great," Jessie said. "And thanks."

"So I guess we know who's to blame for the Articles of Faith test," Hannah said.

"I made a suggestion, and the Young Women's leaders seemed to think it was a good one," Joe said, still looking at Mo. "I'm glad you had a good time."

Just then his brother Mark bounded up to him, almost knocking him over. They began to walk toward the parking lot.

"See ya later, Joe," Hannah said. Then she told her two best friends, "He's sure a good dancer."

Jessie nodded. "Yeah, and easy to talk to."

They obviously hadn't noticed that Mo hadn't danced with him once.

Tyrone walked up to them. He chatted with the group for a few minutes, then said to Mo, "I'm glad you came."

She smiled. "I had a good time."

Hannah and Jessie were talking to a girl from another ward. Tyrone stepped a little closer to Mo. "Hey, what if I call you sometime?"

"Um, yeah, that would be nice."

"I'll look up your number in the church directory. What's your mom and dad's name?"

Mo's voice caught in her throat. "It's . . . it's probably just under my mom's name. Kate Matheson."

"Okay. Got it," he said, tapping his temple as if that would help him remember.

His friend went by and grabbed his arm. "Ready to go?"

"If I have to," Tyrone said, then shot a smile in Mo's direction. "See ya later."

By the time Bailey finally pulled into the almost-deserted parking lot, the three girls were thoroughly chilled but had been afraid to go inside in case she came and they couldn't see her. "We've been waiting for almost an hour," Mo complained as they got in the car.

"I'm sorry," Bailey growled, obviously not very sorry. "Some things are more important."

Jessie and Hannah fell asleep about a half hour into the drive, so Mo said to Bailey, "How did it go? Tell me everything."

"I got lost and it took me quite a while to find the right building. It's pretty close to Whyte Avenue, and there were a lot of people hanging out there in the evening. Lots of bars. Lots of loud people." Bailey paused. "It didn't seem like a good place for a family."

"Brooke is little, though," Mo said. "It's not like she is out riding her bike down the street or walking to the corner store for some candy."

Bailey shuddered. "Not yet."

"But you found the right apartment?"

Bailey's shoulders drooped, and she glanced over at Mo. "It was so run-down looking, Maury. Big pieces of stucco chipping off the building. The halls smelled like cigarette smoke, and there were holes in the walls.

"I had to ring the buzzer twice before Laura answered. Even talking through the intercom, she sounded stressed, and not like herself at all. When I first got in the apartment, she pretended everything was fine, but her eyes were all red and her hair was a mess.

"I asked her if she was okay, and she said she'd had a rough day. She said I should have let her know I was coming."

"But you've left messages on her answering machine and she hasn't called you back," Mo said.

"Exactly! That's what I told her."

Bailey looked into the rearview mirror as if checking to see that Hannah and Jessie were still asleep. Mo turned and realized Hannah was even snoring softly.

"Well, Laura kind of snapped at me after that," Bailey continued. "She said there's been a lot going on right now and she hasn't had time to—"

"How long does it take to make a quick phone call?" Mo interrupted.

"I know. But she said she was really stressed out and everything is going to be fine. I started to think that maybe Brooke wasn't sleeping as I had assumed. Maybe something happened to her. It's like I could sense it in the apartment, that we were totally and completely alone. And I was right. Brooke wasn't there, Maury. She was at Laura's mother's house."

Mo's hand came to her throat. "How come?"

"Oh, she tried to make it sound like it was just a fun visit with Grandma. Laura went to the kitchen and brought us each a glass of lemonade, and we sat on the couch. I wanted to shake her and say, 'What's going on?' I mean, her mother lives in Wetaskiwin."

"How far is that from Edmonton? An hour and a half?"

"Something like that. I was going crazy, Maury. I knew there was something she wasn't telling me. Then she started crying."

Mo could hardly swallow. "Is something wrong with Brooke?"

"She's fine. It has nothing to do with Brooke. It's Tom. His business went under."

"Oh no."

"Now he has the chance to work with a company that does consulting or something, but it's in Saudi Arabia. He'd be traveling around so much that Laura would be alone most of the time, and she's worried about living there. Women have all these restrictions there about going out in public without a man, and covering their heads and . . ." Bailey looked over at Mo. "It's a dangerous place. Plus Laura just got accepted in an art program with some big-time artist I've never heard of. She's wanted to study with this lady since she was in high school. The artist is super picky about who she'll work with, and Laura had to send a portfolio. She's tried three times and was finally accepted."

"What are they going to do?"

"Tom is going to take the job. Laura said it was only for the next nine months and he'll come back to Canada between projects, every couple of months."

"Wow."

"Laura kept saying, 'It will be hard, but it won't be forever.'"

"Is he in Saudi Arabia now?" Mo asked.

"No. He's doing some training first." Bailey slapped her open palms on the steering wheel. "This isn't the way things were supposed to turn out."

"I guess he has to go where the job is."

Bailey shook her head. "He's basically abandoning his family."

"That's not true."

"Nine months? That's practically a year. When Laura applied for the art thing, she thought he'd be home with Brooke in the evenings while she was away, but he'll be gone."

"What a mess," Mo said.

Bailey chewed her lip, and in the lights from the dashboard, Mo saw something in her face. "What?" Mo said.

"I told her I'd be her roommate. I'll watch Brooke when she's at class."

"What?"

"I was thinking of moving to Edmonton when I graduate anyway. She'll charge me next to nothing for rent. And I'll love Brooke as much as she does."

"That's months away."

"Her parents can help her out for a while longer."

"This isn't up to you to fix," Mo said.

"It helps me as much as it helps her. I want to do it."

Mo just nodded. This was the opposite of their mom's advice that Bailey should move on.

18

Nathan and Sarah's Special Date

Nathan wanted to do something special for Sarah. On the way to the weekly youth activity, he said to Maury and Bailey, "What would be a cool date, something that would stand out?"

"You and Sarah have been dating longer than I realized," Maury said. She was sitting in the front passenger seat.

"Uh-huh," he said. "Officially dating for a couple months." He smirked to himself, wondering how that would match up with Sarah's tally.

"Has this been in groups?" Mo's accusation rang with echoes of Nathan's suggestion that she only date in groups.

He thought of all the people at the bowling alley. "Sometimes." It was lame. They had been on a single date, even then.

"And it seems pretty 'steady' too," Maury added.

"It is steady," Nathan admitted. "I'm a lot older than you are. She is . . . " He stopped. He wasn't going to praise Sarah to his sisters. They'd either think he was a geek or tease him mercilessly. "I'm going to be gone for two years." Maury folded her arms but didn't say more.

From the back seat, Bailey said. "So you're looking for something unique for you both to think back on when you're gone on your mission."

Nathan met her eyes in the rearview mirror. "Exactly."

"How much can you spend?"

"Quite a bit. Most of our dates cost nothing." They had gone on bike rides, and every week they watched a favorite television show together that he recorded. Mostly, though, they spent time talking— so much that now she was his best friend as well as his girlfriend.

"Then I have the perfect idea."

When Bailey finished telling him her thoughts, Nathan smiled and said, "That *is* perfect!"

Nathan drove to Sarah's house on a sunny Saturday afternoon in the first week of June. Her father answered the door and nodded at him curtly. "Nathan."

"Hello, Mr. Marshall," Nathan replied.

Sarah patted her father's arm and slipped out onto the porch with Nathan.

"Nice day," Mrs. Marshall said, appearing at her husband's side.

"Very nice," Nathan agreed.

"Goodbye!" Sarah told her parents in a sweet tone. The purple dress she wore came in at the waist and swished when she walked. She had a white sweater over her arm. Her dark-brown hair glimmered with red tones in the sunshine as she and Nathan headed to the car. He opened the door for her, and as she got in, he whispered, "You look beautiful."

She looked up at him. "Thanks. You clean up pretty good yourself, Matheson."

Nathan adjusted his tie. He hadn't worn the blue shirt with white pinstripes since graduation. He always wore a white shirt to church.

On the way to Edmonton, he and Sarah sang along to the radio. When Nathan sang the wrong words, she laughed and corrected him. It was so fun to hear her giggle and ask, "What did you say? What does that mean?" that he sometimes sang the wrong words on purpose.

"I didn't know there were riverboat cruises up the North Saskatchewan River," Sarah said as they pulled into the parking lot at the dock.

"Neither did I," said Nathan. "Bailey told me about it when I mentioned I was looking for something special."

"Any time I spend with you is special," Sarah said.

Nathan put the car in park and leaned over and kissed her. She was so real, so down to earth. She didn't need fancy, expensive dates, but that's what made this even more extraordinary to share with her.

They boarded the riverboat, and Nathan held Sarah's hand. "Let's check out all the decks." People on the first deck were getting cocktails and choosing seats for dinner. Nathan led Sarah through the large open room and out onto the small deck that circled the riverboat.

"Edmonton is such a pretty city," she said. "There are so many more trees than in Calgary."

"You always notice the good. In things, in people."

She smiled. "It's a gorgeous warm evening, and I'm on a river cruise with my boyfriend. You're judging me on a good night."

"It's not just today. You give things a chance." Nathan turned and faced her. "The only thing you really haven't given a chance is my church."

The boat was pulling out of the dock, and Sarah looked out over the water. "You can be religious without a church," she said.

"Then you do believe in God?"

"Yes, I guess I do."

"And Jesus?"

"Sure. Why not? I could believe in Jesus. But don't tell my parents I said that."

After a pause, Nathan said, "I think it's important to know who we are and where we came from. My church teaches that we lived in the spirit world before we came to earth."

"The pre-mortal world," Sarah said. "You talked about that before."

"You know I'm going on a mission, but I don't think you realize how important the truths of the gospel are to me."

She laid her hand on his back. "I know how passionate you are about it, Nathan. I think that's great."

"Great for me, but not for you?"

She leaned in and kissed his cheek. "Let's not talk about this now, okay?"

He had planned for this day to be a perfect memory, so maybe it was best not to launch into a discussion of the mission of Jesus Christ, and the restoration of the true Church. "Yeah, okay," Nathan said.

They stepped into the main dining area, but it was pretty hectic with so many conversations going on all at once, so Nathan told Sarah, "Let's check out the second deck." They climbed the narrow steps. Only about half of the tables here were occupied. Chefs dressed in white were bringing food to a buffet table at the front.

The Edmonton skyline floated past as Sarah and Nathan ate roast beef, chicken, and a wide variety of salads and vegetables. At one point he looked at his half-empty plate and couldn't remember tasting anything. *This was crazy.* He had a testimony of the Church. He wanted to get married in the temple someday, have children, and raise them to be active in the Church. And here he was falling for a girl who wouldn't come to church meetings and who said she *could* believe in Jesus Christ, as if it really wasn't a big deal whether she did or not.

"This has to be the best gravy in the world," Sarah said suddenly.

"Uh-huh," Nathan mumbled. Sarah was sweet and had such an open heart. The Spirit would work on her, and then Sarah's values and faith would line up with Nathan's. At least he could hope.

"Let's go outside for a bit," Sarah suggested when they had finished their main meal.

The sun was dipping low, transforming the sky into a magical landscape of pink and orange hues. Nathan and Sarah leaned against the railing. The boat hummed with the workings of the engine. "It's so pretty," Sarah said.

"You're so pretty." Nathan wrapped his arm around her waist, and her arm came around his.

"I wish I knew what the future held," she whispered.

"I was thinking that too, but I've changed my mind. What would be the fun in living a story you've already read?"

"I suppose. But if a story is especially sad in the middle, I sometimes skip to the end to make sure everything is going to turn out well." Sarah smiled. "I only read stories that end well."

Nathan chuckled. "That's not very adventurous." She turned to face him, and he held her in his arms. "Sometimes you just have to enjoy the moment," he said. "And trust . . . and hope."

"I guess I can do that." She turned back so she was facing the riverbank gliding by. Eventually, she said, "We should go get our dessert before they take it away."

They went into the covered area, and Nathan took a dessert plate from the stack. "They look amazing," Sarah said, picking up a chocolate square with a fancy design in white on top and setting it on his plate. He added a couple of tarts, and she added another square. Music began on the lower deck. "Sounds like the dance is starting," said Nathan.

They finished their desserts sitting side by side, sharing off the single plate, and watching the glowing orb of the sun dip below the horizon. It was like saying goodbye to this stage of Nathan's life, the pre-mission life.

Not yet, thought Nathan. *Not quite yet.*

He stood and took Sarah's hand and led her down the narrow stairway to the dance floor. It was a rowdier crowd on the first level to match the music. They stayed along the fringe and danced to rock music, country two-step beats, and even a couple of line dances. Nathan didn't know the line dances very well but did his best to copy Sarah.

"Ready for some air?" asked Nathan after about an hour.

Sarah grinned. "Yeah, that would be nice."

They filled a couple of glasses with ice water from the clear dispensers down the center of the floor and took them out on the deck. Sarah's features were illuminated by the outside lighting. When she shivered, Nathan asked if she wanted her sweater.

"I left it on the chair over there." She indicated a chair along the edge of the dance floor.

"I'll be right back."

He went on the errand, feeling fully like a boyfriend. Not just any boyfriend, but the boyfriend of a wonderful girl. He returned to Sarah and helped her slip her sweater on. Then he put his arm around her shoulder. "For added warmth," he said.

She leaned against him. "That's very chivalrous of you."

"The boat has turned around. I didn't notice while we were dancing."

"I wonder how many stars we could see if there weren't so many city lights," Sarah commented. "I know some constellations."

"I know the Big Dipper," said Nathan. "I heard it called the Big Bear, and the Little Dipper was called the Little Bear. That threw me off when I was a kid."

"I can understand that. A dipper, yes. A bear—well, you've got to really use your imagination."

The DJ called, "We're nearing the end of the cruise. Thank you for journeying with us this evening. We hope you've had a great time. This will be our last dance."

"This has been really nice," Sarah told Nathan.

"Yeah, it has. One more dance?"

Sarah nodded, and he led her to the dance floor. It was a slow, romantic song. As they swayed together, the hemline of her dress swished against his leg. She was beautiful and kind. If only she would give the Church a chance, she would be perfect. He had given her a Book of Mormon and she'd accepted it as a gift, one that she had to hide away from her parents in a drawer where it would probably be forgotten. She would talk about pre-mortal life and the plan of salvation, but as soon as he brought up going to church she closed off. His heart fell at the thought.

"What is it?" Sarah asked as the song came to an end. She was looking into Nathan's eyes.

"Nothing. I'm just sorry the evening is over."

"So am I. This was an excellent idea."

He kissed her cheek.

They held hands as he drove back to St. Paul. Once they were far enough from the city lights, Sarah pointed out the constellations in the dark sky.

Nathan's eyelids were heavy by the time they arrived in St. Paul. He walked Sarah to her front door. They shared a kiss and he said, "Good-night, Sarah."

She threw her arms around his neck. "Tonight was totally magical. Thank you."

19

The First Float

The ball was about five feet in diameter. Joe and his brother stayed on either side to keep the wind from blowing the ball across the lawn. Mo, Hannah, and Jessie stood watching with the other young men and young women.

"Your joint activities are always the best," Jessie told Mo. "Even if it does make me think of marijuana."

Joe's hair stood on end in the wind and then rumpled as though the breeze wanted to pause and run its fingers through it. "It's called 'joint' because it's both boys and girls together," Mo muttered without looking at Jessie.

"They're ready to pray," Hannah whispered.

After the opening prayer, Sister Hall, the new Young Women president, helped the men position the volleyball net. "That should give both sides plenty of room," she said.

"Count them off," suggested Brother Peterson, from the Young Men presidency.

Sister Hall counted off "One, two; one, two; one, two . . ." Joe was a one. Mo was a two.

Mark ran off to join the group of two's on the other side of the net. Mo followed him. The wind picked up, and the huge ball rolled quickly toward the baseball diamond at the back of the park. Mo ran with a few others and got behind the ball. Joe was next to her as they pushed it back to the volleyball net. "Thank you," he said coolly, looking her in the eye. Their hands were less than six inches apart on the inflatable ball.

Mo and Joe had been so close once, but now he spoke to her like she was a stranger. With a lump in her throat, Mo nodded. When they reached the net, Mo walked to the other side with her team.

The large ball was launched over the net toward her. Mo and seven or eight of her teammates got under it and pushed against it, lifting as one. It rose almost straight above them. When it sank down, they jumped and lobbed it over the net.

Joe said something to Hannah, who stood beside him. They laughed. Mo watched them on and off throughout the game. Once, the ball flew over the net and knocked Joe and Hannah to the grass, but they managed to hit the ball and keep it alive. Jessie got under it with other kids on their side and sent it in a huge arc toward Mo's team. Joe came over to Jessie and congratulated her on the play.

After a while, Brother Peterson called, "Time for refreshments. The guys with jobs need to come with me." Joe was among those who hurried ahead of the group.

Mo met Hannah and Jessie. "I hope my thumb's not sprained," said Jessie, shaking her hand as they crossed the lawn.

Hannah laughed. "Way to take one for the team!"

"That was fun," Jessie said.

In the gym, Joe stood behind a small table. He pulled the lid off a bucket of vanilla ice cream, grabbed a metal scoop, and dug out a large ball of ice cream. Several people waited in front of the table. Mo, Jessie, and Hannah joined the others waiting for ice cream. Joe's brother Mark poured a glass of root beer, and Joe plopped the ice cream in. It started to foam. Joe handed the first float to Mo, met her eyes briefly, and then went back to scooping ice cream.

A half hour later, when the floats were all gone and the basketballs had been stowed away, Hannah and Jessie piled into the little Toyota. Mo backed the car out of the parking spot. "I noticed who got the first float," Hannah said in a singsong tone.

"Just lucky," Mo replied.

"Joe asked me how often you and Tyrone have phone dates," Jessie said.

Mo frowned. "Phone dates?"

"That's what he called them."

"What did you tell him?"

Jessie shrugged. "I said I didn't know for sure but you talked to him every week or two."

"What did he say to that?" Hannah asked.

"Nothing."

"It's none of his business anyway," Mo said, then changed the subject. "That activity was fun, though. We should do that for one of the joints we have to plan. I wonder where they got that ball."

The girls talked about the game until Mo dropped Jessie off. Then Hannah said, "Are you still mad at Joe?"

"No, not mad, exactly. I just don't want to be in the kind of relationship where somebody thinks he can restrict me and control me. Do you know what I mean?"

"If that's really what he was doing, then yes."

Mo exhaled. "Part of me misses him and wants to just forget it."

"And if he apologized?"

Mo pulled to the curb in front of Hannah's house. "I don't know. Actions speak louder than words."

"And he's made no effort," Hannah replied. She opened her door. "Except he did give you the first float."

The words hung in the air for a moment before Hannah said goodbye.

20

Bailey's Plans Revealed

Mo finished ten reps of bicep curls with her hand weights, then strapped on the ankle weights. "You're going to get muscle-bound," Bailey, said looking up from a clothing catalog.

"No, I won't. I just need to be stronger so I don't get pushed around under the basket so much."

When Mo finished, she put the weights away behind the couch. Bailey made a *hmph* sort of noise. Mo looked over her shoulder. "You found some dresses formal enough for graduation?"

"There are so few," Bailey said. "What if three girls are wearing the same dress?"

Mo pointed at a deep orange one. "That's kind of nice."

Bailey rocked in the rocking chair as she seemed to consider the dress. "It's too clingy."

"It's not bad."

"In the stomach area it is, and that's not a good area for me."

"You look good," Mo said.

"I exercise but I don't think my stomach will ever be flat like it was."

"It's tougher for some women after having a baby. Don't be hard on yourself. You are eating right and working out. That's all you can do."

Bailey shook her head. "I know but I'm still not going to wear a dress that's form-fitting in the tummy."

"Do I get to go to the banquet?"

"I'm not sure how many tickets Mom wants to buy. I think she was getting enough for the whole family, but I don't know. They're kind of expensive."

"Do you have a date yet?" Mo asked.

"I'm going alone."

"What about Roy?"

"No."

"I thought he asked you."

Bailey closed the catalog and dropped it on the floor by the chair. "He did. I said no."

"Why? Maybe he's not the best-looking guy in the world, but he's kind of cute."

"It's not his looks, Maury."

"Then what?"

"I don't need a guy—I'd rather go by myself. I did the work. I'm graduating. I don't need some guy I hardly know in a bunch of pictures with me. They're all jerks deep down, anyway."

"I want to punch Wade right now," Mo said crossly. "I mean, every guy is not like him!"

"That's easy for you to say right now, Maury. You have Joe Parker taking you on fun group dates, and phone calls from that Tyrone guy from the stake dance, plus movie dates with what's-his-name from work."

"Garrett."

"So, you're just kind of on the surface. You're out having fun. And great—more power to you. But past the surface . . . watch out."

The sisters were quiet for a moment, and then Mo said, "Joe and I had a fight. We haven't gone out or even really talked for months."

"What did he do?"

"It was when we went painting in Edmonton. He acted stupid. He was jealous and possessive because I talked to his cousin.

Tyrone is Joe's cousin, remember? Well, I won't have some guy telling me who I can talk to and what I can do."

"See what I mean," Bailey said with a sad-but-triumphant tone. "Even Joe Parker turned into a nut case."

"It *was* crazy."

Nathan entered the living room with a sandwich. "Or maybe he's crazy about Maury."

"Since when do you stick up for Joe?" Mo said.

"Since I met Garrett."

Mo laughed, but there was truth in Nathan's statement. Garrett was obviously more streetwise than Joe. Garrett was a little too laid back about a lot of things, too, and Mo even suspected that he had done drugs before. He had made a reference to some sort of drug paraphernalia, and Mo didn't understand so he had to explain it to her. Knowing about drug stuff didn't mean he actually did drugs, but he might have. Mo and he were just friends, though, and the "dates" Bailey was referring to were really a group of McDonald's employees all going to a movie together. Mo had insisted on group dates, and that was Garrett's solution.

Jordy jumped onto Nathan's back and asked, "Want to play foosball?"

"Okay," Nathan agreed.

"Best garage sale find of the summer," Mom said as she entered the living room as the two boys were leaving. "Did you find a dress in the catalog, Bailey? We can send it back if it doesn't fit, but we better order soon."

"There's nothing," Bailey said.

"Let's go in to the city this weekend," Mom suggested. "Where's the newspaper?" She spotted it on the coffee table under Mo's sprawling homework. "We can look at housing while we're there, too. We need to get something in place for September. I marked the ones close to the university, and we can take a look at on-campus housing."

Mo glanced at Bailey, who said, "I've already found a place to stay. I've looked into the bus routes, and I'll be able to get to the university without much trouble. And hopefully, I can find a job close by until school starts. So, it's all settled." "Why didn't you tell me before?" Mom asked. "You know I've been looking for apartments. Where is it? Can you afford it alone?"

"I won't be alone, I'll have a roommate."

"Who? Another LDS girl, or a few of them?" When Bailey didn't answer, Mom continued, "It would be best to be with other Church girls, then you can go to activities and Church meetings together."

Bailey swallowed. "I'm going to move in with Laura Anderson."

Mom gave a little gasp and walked over to sit gingerly on the sofa. "That doesn't seem right, Bailey," she began slowly. "They don't have a basement suite, do they? No, they live in an apartment. We'll look when we go shopping, and I'm sure we'll be able to find something better." Mom raised her eyebrows knowingly.

"Tom will hardly be there," Bailey said. After spilling the whole story, she explained, "I'll get to see Brooke every day and help with babysitting. There are three bedrooms."

Besides a few exclamations and muttering of "Oh, no" behind her hands, Mom had mostly let Bailey tell her tale. When Bailey finished, however, it was as though Mom had been holding back a dam of words. She paced the room in quick, jerky steps. "You can't be serious, Bailey. You've got to let the past go! You can't hang on to it, or it's going to completely ruin your life."

"How can you say that? Sharing an apartment isn't going to ruin my life. Brooke needs me. Laura needs me."

"Lots of people have to make sacrifices, and if Tom and Laura feel he needs to take this job, that's their business. But you don't have to solve their babysitting issues. For heaven's sakes, Bailey, break free. How are you going to have a normal college life living far from campus, not having a vehicle, and living with a baby?"

"It's what I want," Bailey said simply. Then after a moment, she added, "It's helping me, too."

"Think about it rationally for a moment." Mom's face was red, and she didn't appear too rational herself. "Suppose you meet a nice guy in one of your classes. He suggests you study together at your apartment. You take him back there, and what does he find? You sharing an apartment with a mother and her baby? Are you going to tell him that Brooke was your child that you gave up for adoption? Can't you see, Bailey? This way, it will always be in your face. I'm not saying you don't tell anyone, but is it really the *first* thing you want to tell people?"

Bailey shook her head. "I'm not going to get serious with a guy, but even if I did, I'd tell him about Brooke."

"Of course," Mom said. "Eventually."

"I've already decided," Bailey replied. "I already told Laura. If I can get a job for the summer, I'll move in even sooner."

"It's not wise," Mom said.

A movement out of the corner of her eye caught Mo's attention. Nathan and Jordy were standing at the living room entrance. Nathan looked stunned. Jordy seemed to have noted Nathan's expression and copied it.

The conversation was far from over. Over the next couple of weeks, Mo heard Mom and Bailey talk about it at least twice more. Mom pled with her to reconsider her decision. She listed the reasons it would be inconvenient to not be closer to the university. She explained how Bailey's social life would be hurt both with boys and with girls her own age. Mom offered to help her with rent. She spoke about how Bailey should be leaving her past behind, not dragging it with her. She also said that Bailey would grow more attached to Brooke instead of letting her go. That was actually what Bailey was looking forward to, Mo thought. Bailey seemed to think that was a bonus, not a drawback.

21

Jealousy ... and Fries with That

Nathan stood filling fry boxes and staring at Sarah. She was at the cash register today and looking especially beautiful. A guy at the counter was talking to her. He had already ordered and was just schmoozing. He looked like a guy who'd been talking to Sarah a few days ago, and the same guy she was with at neon bowling. They laughed as they spoke. Nathan clenched his teeth and finished making a teen burger and slipped it into the rack. The guy had perfect, magazine-cover teeth.

He shouldn't act possessive or jealous—that was one thing he learned from Joe Parker's mistake. Maury was so mad at Joe. Sarah set a frosted mug of root beer on the tray in front of the guy. He said something else and she chuckled.

But Nathan *was* jealous. After the last time this guy had chatted her up at the A&W counter, Nathan had asked who he was. Sarah had said the guy was a friend of hers. But obviously, he was totally after her.

The timer went off, and Nathan dumped the crispy fries in the metal bin and filled a cardboard box for the order. "Fries are up," he called when Sarah didn't seem to notice.

"Thanks." She turned toward him and took the fries.

"Any time," Nathan said in a friendly voice. He wasn't about to do anything to cause a rift between them, and jealousy could do exactly that.

Mo helped Bailey with her packing. With each item she added to a cardboard box, another little piece of Mo's heart was pulled away. "You don't have to worry too much if you forget something," she told Bailey. "Mom goes to Edmonton all the time and could bring you stuff."

"I know. But she's so grumpy." Bailey stuffed her makeup bag into the corner of the big suitcase on the floor. "I don't want to ask her to do me favors right now."

Mo held up two dresses and waited. Bailey nodded, meaning she wanted them packed. "Brooke is so cute," Bailey said. "I think it will be great to live with her."

Nathan and Sarah entered Bailey's room. "What else can I take?" asked Nathan. The room seemed so barren without the bed.

Bailey looked up at him. "You got the small dresser from the basement?"

"Yeah."

"Well, that box of shoes is ready." Bailey pointed to the large box beside her closet.

Nathan picked up the box and seemed surprised by the weight. "Why do you have so many shoes?"

Sarah chuckled. "Girls need shoes."

"Nathan totally doesn't get that." Bailey smiled at Sarah.

"What can I do now?" Sarah asked.

Bailey pointed to a pile in the corner. "Sheets, blankets, and pillow," she said.

"I can't believe you're moving to Edmonton," Mo put in. "You just graduated last week."

"And your job starts on the weekend?" Sarah said.

"Yeah." Bailey took a deep breath. "Early shift at the pancake house. But at least it's within walking distance so I won't have to take transit."

Sarah nodded. "What about when school starts? Are you going to take late classes?"

"No. I work the six AM shift now, and I'll have the four thirty shift in September."

"That's perfect." Mo tried to sound enthusiastic.

"What?" Bailey said.

"I'm going to miss you."

Jordy bounded into the room. "CD player?" He pointed at it.

"Yes," Bailey replied.

"Why don't we put a blanket around it in the truck?" Sarah suggested.

"Good idea," Jordy said. Then he whispered to Mo. "She's pretty *and* smart."

Sarah followed Jordy out with one of the blankets.

Passing Sarah on his way into the room, Nathan caught her eye. The look he gave her was peaceful and happy . . . almost serene. It made Mo's heart ache just a bit to see it.

"We need to get going," Nathan told Bailey. "Aren't you finished with that yet?"

She added a stack of four or five shirts and flipped the lid of the suitcase over. "Ready now."

Mo helped her zip the bag, then said, "Email me all the time."

"I will. Laura has a computer, and hopefully, I'll make enough to buy one of my own pretty soon."

Mo carried the suitcase and Bailey grabbed her purse and the last box.

President Harris sat behind the steering wheel of the truck parked out front. The last couple of things were put in the truck bed, and Nathan and Bailey jumped in the back of the extended cab. Mom got in the front. Bailey called through the open window, "I'll miss you, Maury, but we'll email all the time."

Mo waved and they drove away.

"Bye for now," Sarah called on the way to her car.

"Bye," Mo said. She and Jordy went back in the house. She wandered out to the kitchen, then down the hallway and looked into Bailey's deserted room.

"I'm going to Barry's house," Jordy said from behind her.

"Okay, but don't go any farther than next door without asking me first."

Mo went to the computer and wrote Bailey an email.

Two days later, Bailey sent an email reply:

Brooke gets cuter every day! I absolutely love being with her. She's crawling around, and today we played with blocks. I built the tower and she knocked it down. She must have done that twenty times. We took her for her first-ever frozen yogurt yesterday. She loved it. She was absolutely wild for it.

Work is hard. My feet hurt, which I guess I should have expected, being on my feet all day, when I'm not used to that. But guess what? My arms hurt too. Waitresses carry heavy stuff. I'm wimpy, I guess. I'll probably build more muscle than you with your weights. I'll be ready to arm wrestle you in about a month. Bye for now.

22

Secret Beach Plans

Mo took a few potato chips out of the bag and set them on her lap before passing the bag to Hannah and Jessie, who sat in lawn chairs next to hers. The sun warmed Mo's face as she sipped her lemonade.

Jessie bit into a chip. "I haven't seen a more ridiculous separation since my favorite soap-opera characters broke up over the kind of doughnuts they ordered."

"Really?" Mo stretched out the word.

"You and Joe are obviously still into each other," Hannah said.

"But you've spent months hardly talking and intently staring at each other," Jessie pointed out.

"I'm not going to have a guy—" Mo began.

"—tell you who you can talk to, I know," Jessie finished. "But I don't think that's what he was doing. He was jealous of the fun you were having with Tyrone. That's all. What does he act like at church and youth group?" She turned to Hannah.

"You've been to enough activities to see," Hannah replied. "And we can both see it."

Mo frowned. "See what?"

"That you're crazy about each other," Jessie exclaimed. "It's killing you to be apart."

"And what about Tyrone?" asked Hannah.

"We talk quite a bit," Mo said. "His family has some sort of super-good phone plan."

"And . . ." Jessie encouraged.

Mo sighed. "What do you want me to say? We have fun talking. He's cool. He's funny."

Jessie looked at Hannah, and something passed between them.

"You're a lucky girl." Hannah bit her top lip. "Sorry. I know I shouldn't say that." She looked at Jessie. "Not after the fire they had and . . . and everything."

"It's okay," Mo said. "Want to shoot some hoops at the park?".

Hannah finished the last of her lemonade and said, "Let's go."

That evening Jessie called Mo's house. "Beach day tomorrow? It's supposed to be a hot one."

"Sounds fun, and I have the day off," Mo said. "Do you have a car we can take?"

"Yep. And the dinghy. Hannah can come, too."

"Great! That sounds so fun."

"How about if I pick you up at nine thirty?"

"Fine—see you then. Should I bring some sandwiches?"

"Nope. I have it covered."

At nine thirty the next morning, Jessie was at Mo's house with Hannah already riding shotgun. Mo threw her beach bag on the back seat and said, "My mom said I have to ask if you have enough life jackets."

"Of course," Jessie said. "Do you think my dad would let me out in the dinghy without them?"

"Then I'm allowed to go." Mo didn't say what she was thinking—that Jessie's dad wouldn't care whether or not Jessie wore a life jacket going over Niagara Falls. He was very casual about things including safety, school attendance, and having enough gas in his car. It was always empty, and anytime he let Jessie borrow it, she had to stop at a gas station. On two different days, she and her friends had run out of gas on the way to the gas station.

Jessie pulled up to the gas pump, and Hannah and Mo handed her some money. "Thanks," she said.

"How much do we owe for the food?" Mo asked.

Jessie shook her head. "Nothing. It was stuff we had around the house."

"Which lake are we going to?" Hannah asked.

"West Cove is close," Jessie said.

"I like Long Lake better," Mo said.

Hannah looked over her shoulder. "I vote West Cove too."

Mo shrugged. "Okay. I have sunscreen. It's supposed to be really hot this afternoon."

"Classic!" Jessie looked over at Hannah, smiled, and got out to pump the gas.

Just under half an hour later Jessie pulled to a stop in a parking stall close to the beach. The girls got out of the car and pulled the folded dinghy out of the trunk. "Are you sure this is a three-person boat?" Mo asked.

"That's what it said on the box," Jessie replied. "But it would have to be some small people."

They left the boat on the beach and walked back to the car. Mo grabbed Jessie's bag along with her own, and Jessie carried the pump back to the shore. "I'll take the first shift," said Jessie, positioning the nozzle in the dinghy. The pump was a tall cylinder with a place for a person's feet at the bottom, and a handle at the top. After a couple of minutes, Jessie was out of breath, so Mo took a turn. "It's sticky," said Jessie. "I don't remember it being this hard to pump last year."

Movement caught Mo's eye as she passed off the pump to Hannah. A dusty brown Suburban had parked next to their car. Two boys climbed out. "That looks like Robert and Darius," Mo said.

Jessie looked up. "Is it?"

The boys went to the back of the vehicle and pulled out a much larger dinghy that was already inflated.

Then Mo saw Joe. He stood at the front of the vehicle, staring at the girls. Her breath caught in her throat. "And Joe is with them," she mumbled.

"Hmm," Jessie said, obviously not surprised. "Here, it's your turn." She stepped to the side, and Mo moved into her spot to pump.

"Wow, I don't believe it," Hannah said. "This is such a crazy coincidence. I mean it is the closest lake to town and all, but there are lots of others to choose from, and this early, to be here, at the same time.

They were the only ones on the beach, and it was nice and warm already. Sweat ran down the back of Mo's neck as she worked to finish pumping up the boat.

"I'll pump," Hannah told her.

The boys approached laden down with blankets and the dinghy. Mo's heart jumped at the sight of Joe. Then she reminded herself of his possessiveness. She didn't need a control freak in her life, even one as cute as Joe Parker.

Suddenly it dawned on her. "Jessie, did you do this?"

Jessie sighed. "Don't be mad."

"Of course I'm mad," Mo hissed. "I don't want to hang out with them all day. I don't want to fall for Joe again." She gave Jessie a look. "My heart may say yes, but my head says no. And I don't want to be stupid."

"They're our friends too," Hannah put in.

Mo huffed. "Fine! Whatever!"

She took another turn at the pump. Soon she was breathing hard and handing off the pump to Hannah. That pump used muscles Mo apparently wasn't used to using, and her shoulders were getting sore.

The guys had stopped and were filling their dinghy with towels. Mo turned and looked out over the lake. The few lazy clouds overhead were prodded along by a light breeze high above.

Joe held the back end of the boat as the boys moved closer to the girls. Robert was in the lead, and he tripped in the sand. The other two boys tumbled down after him. The boat bounced on Robert's body and sprung ahead. Mo couldn't help but laugh.

"How's that for an entrance?" called Robert, standing and brushing sand off his bare chest.

"Graceful," Jessie yelled.

Joe and Darius scrambled to their feet. Darius rubbed his chin. Hannah chuckled. "That was hilarious." She glanced at Mo and said, "Your turn, Maury," then stepped away from the pump.

Without a word, Joe took Hannah's place at the pump. Mo whispered thanks and stretched her tight shoulders. The breeze cooled the sweat on her back. For a small dinghy, this thing sure seemed to need a lot of air.

"It's a great day to hang out at the beach," Robert said.

Joe finished filling the dinghy, and Mo helped him screw the plug into place. "Well, looks like you're ready to roll," Joe said.

"Ready to *float*," Mo corrected.

"Totally ready," Darius said. Then, as if that was a prearranged cue, Robert, Darius, Hannah, and Jessie grabbed the large boat and headed for the water, leaving Joe and Mo behind.

"You two take the small one," Jessie shouted. "It's too small for three people anyway."

Darius turned and shot a goofy grin to Mo and Joe, then called out, "But perfect for two."

23

Enchanted Dinghy?

"What's going on?" Mo asked softly.

"Do you think I know?" Joe said. They stood staring at their friends for a moment. Then Joe said, "They forgot their life jackets."

The group of four was already a few feet from the shore and paddling as if trying to escape a zombie invasion. "We could row the jackets out to them," Joe suggested.

"Okay," Mo said.

They threw the life jackets into the tiny dinghy. "There's hardly room for us," Joe said as he and Mo climbed in and cast off into the lake. They each took an oar and rowed the dinghy forward.

As they neared the other boat, their friends' paddling became more furious and the distance between them increased. "I think they're avoiding us," Mo said.

"We're not going to catch them." Joe took the long length of rope at the front of the dinghy, looped the extra life jackets through it, and tied the rope. Then he dropped the life jackets over the side of the boat. The colorful jackets reminded Mo of the tail of a kite.

Joe leaned back and closed his eyes. The glow of the sun washed over him. "I guess they figure we need to be alone." He looked so cute, with a smudge of wet sand on his cheek.

Mo didn't say anything, and after a little while Joe asked, "So, how are things going with Tyrone?" Then he sat straighter and exclaimed, "Strike that. Forget I said anything. It's not my business."

"You're right, it's not," Mo said.

They floated aimlessly, neither of them rowing. "He tells me all the time how great you guys are getting along," Joe said, "and how big his phone bills are, and how phone dates are great, and how you really get to know someone when you talk all the time. I don't think he and I have talked so much in years."

"Really?" Mo said, her mind making connections.

Joe opened his eyes and leaned forward. The deep green of the water made his blue eyes gleam in contrast. "Tyrone really likes you." Joe's smile was sad. "But I hope you and I can at least go back to being good friends. I miss you, Mo. I know I've been a jealous jerk, but I think I'm ready to handle you and Tyrone. You can have a boyfriend and we can still be friends, don't you think?"

"I'm not sure you have it all straight," Mo said.

"What do you mean?"

"Well, Tyrone does call quite a bit and everything, but I wouldn't call him my boyfriend. I wouldn't call *anyone* my boyfriend."

"Hmm." Joe nodded as if this was not a huge revelation. Then he took up the oars and rowed toward the middle of the lake. The other boat was about the size of a basketball from where they were. "Well, are you going to forgive me for the jealous jerk routine?"

"I guess," Mo said.

"You're still mad."

"I want you to know right now, Joe Parker, that no guy is going to boss me around and control my friendships. That's not the kind of relationship I want."

"I wasn't doing that. I was . . . well, I'm kind of crazy about you. You make me act crazy."

"That's not a good excuse!"

Joe looked surprised by the force of her comment. A hundred emotions seemed to skirt over his features before he turned back to the oars. Then his face went red as if he was embarrassed. Suddenly, it occurred to Mo that he had taken a risk to tell her how much he liked her, and she had thrown it back in his face.

"Joe—"

"The thought of Tyrone with you does make me crazy, but not in any sort of, I don't know, unusual way." His eyebrow dipped low as he thought. "Just in a sad, aching kind of way. Not a bossy, controlling way." Joe swallowed and his expression became intense. "You and I have known each other long enough that you must know these things about me. But maybe you don't. I've heard of guys that get mad if their girlfriends go out with their friends. My mom and dad were even talking once about someone who got mad at his wife for reading novels. He thought she should read more important types of books, so she felt pressured to give up the books she liked." His eyebrow twitched. "I'd never be like that. Who was he to tell her what she could read?" He looked past her, seemingly at nothing. "You should be . . . cautious. And if you don't start watching for qualities that could spell danger while you're dating, when are you supposed to start?" After a pause, he said, "You're right. It's not a good enough excuse. You can't be bossy because you like someone." There was another long pause before he continued, "But I'm no bully."

That was true. A warm glow filled Mo that had nothing to do with the summer day. Mo remembered one-on-one basketball with Joe back in the days when she used to beat him. She remembered the first mojo candy he ever gave her; it was orange. She remembered the teddy bear he gave Jordy when he had such awful allergic reactions to coconut, and how she had held that against Joe for so long. She remembered the basketball shoes

Joe gave her after all her belongings were lost in the fire. She remembered his tenderness in helping Sister Andrews last year when she was pregnant. And Mo remembered his concern for her after Dad died. "Okay, Joe," she said finally.

"Okay, you believe me? Or okay, you forgive me?"

"Both," she said, then scooped up a handful of water and tossed it into Joe's face.

He shook his hair. "Thanks, I needed that. I was starting to think you liked me or something." He grabbed one of the oars and created a wave that spilled over the side of the boat and into Mo's lap.

She squealed and splashed him back. The water became a churning chaos of waves. Suddenly, the sound of whooping and hollering drew Mo's attention. Joe looked, too. The other boat was approaching, and their friends were yelling and patting each other on the back. "What's with them?" asked Mo, water dripping from her chin.

"I'm afraid to guess." Joe fit both the paddles in the oarlocks and rowed toward the oncoming boat. When they were in range, he used his paddles to spray their friends.

Suddenly, Robert was in the water and closing the distance between the boats with slow, even strides. He propelled himself up the side of the small dinghy and reached for Joe. Joe ducked and pushed Robert away. All was silent around the boat until Robert sprang from a new spot, grabbed Mo, and pulled her over the side.

She snatched a breath before she went under. A few seconds later, she popped to the surface with her life jacket up at her chin and ears. "That was . . ."

"Great?" Robert said.

Mo grabbed the edge of the dinghy.

"Cool and refreshing?" Robert said, treading water.

"I wish someone hadn't stolen my life jacket," Hannah remarked.

"Stolen?" Joe said, then helped Mo climb back into the small dinghy.

"We went back to shore for them, and they were gone," Darius explained.

Joe pointed to the line of life jackets floating behind the dinghy.

"I think I found the thief," Robert said, still treading water. She always thought of him as being a little awkward and slightly goofy-looking, but he was pretty graceful in the water.

Joe untied the life jackets and threw one to Robert, and the rest to the other boat. As soon as the last zipper was zipped, Joe resumed the water fight with added intensity. He gave Mo one of the oars, and she soon had the hang of creating a good spray with it.

Eventually, all the friends jumped overboard and floated on their backs, each with a hand on the rope of one of the dinghies.

"What did you do that for, Joe?" Darius asked after a few minutes. "We were just coming to say hello."

"That was for the binoculars," Joe replied.

"Binoculars?" Mo said. "What binoculars?"

"Yeah, what binoculars?" Hannah asked. Then she quickly added, "It was Robert's idea!"

"Well, you didn't expect us to just float around for hours not knowing if you two were making up or not," Robert said.

"He has a point," Darius said. "Think of the water fight you two were having. Without the binoculars we wouldn't have known if it was a fun fight or a real fight."

"Invasion of privacy!" Mo yelled.

Darius laughed. "Done out of loving concern."

"You jerk," Joe said, but he was laughing.

"Let's go have some lunch," Jessie suggested.

Mo was next to the large dinghy, so she chose that one. The sides were higher and she got part way up before slipping back into the water. She felt like a beached whale, and it took two more tries and Joe's and Hannah's help to finally get in.

"It's your sunscreen." Hannah giggled. "You're slicked up."

Darius laughed but then said, "You could use some, Hannah. Your shoulders are red."

Robert and Jessie were in the small dinghy. Joe and Darius rowed the large one back to shore at a leisurely pace. It really was a nice day, and Mo felt as light as the breeze after making up with Joe. As they neared the shore, she jumped out with the others and pulled the boat several feet onto the beach.

Robert and Jessie were slower than the others. "What is that *The Love Boat*?" Darius asked, looking through the binoculars at them. "Maybe you and I should take it out after lunch," he said to Hannah, giving her a couple of eyebrow waves.

Hannah stepped back. "That's okay. I'm good."

Darius lifted the binoculars again and gasped.

"What?" Hannah said.

"They're kissing!"

"What?" Hannah reached for the binoculars. "This I gotta see." They passed them around. When it was Mo's turn, she had a perfect view of Robert and Jessie with their lips together. She was happy for them, but just a little jealous that she and Joe hadn't shared a kiss when they made up. As she handed the binoculars to Joe, she said, "This is poetic justice. He who lives by the binoculars, dies by the binoculars!"

"They're coming in," Joe said. When Jessie and Robert were within earshot, Darius, Joe, and Hannah clapped and called out to them, while Mo laughed and waved the binoculars back and forth in the air.

"You guys are scum," Robert said as he pulled the dinghy on shore. He walked over to Mo and reclaimed the binoculars. "Scum."

Jessie smiled. "Turnabout is fair play."

24

All's Well

"We just wanted to make sure you two weren't fighting on the way in," Mo told Robert.

"And you weren't," Joe said. "Not at all."

"You're looking at little red there, buddy," Darius said. "I think you got a bit of a sunburn."

"Invasion of privacy," Robert mumbled.

"Let's go get the cooler," Joe told him.

Robert looked thankful for the diversion. Before leaving the group, he glanced at Jessie and mouthed the word "sorry."

"I'm not," she whispered, smiling back at him.

Darius's cooler was full of ice, soda, and green grapes. Jessie's cooler had sandwiches on Kaiser buns, a jar of dill pickles, and a bag of two-bite-brownies. Everyone spread out their beach towels and blankets, sat in a circle, and dug into the food.

"No wonder you offered to bring lunch," Joe said to Darius. "You had Jessie do all the work."

"I went to the store and bought drinks," Darius said defensively. "And grapes."

"I asked him to bring pop and fruit," Jessie said.

"What? Grapes are fruit," Darius replied. "Did you expect an assortment?"

They bantered back and forth until Mo commented that everything tasted great.

"Grapes are actually the most refreshing choice you could have made," Joe said.

They talked and laughed and relived the best moments of the water fight. Only Robert was quieter than usual.

When the lunch things were packed away, everybody reapplied sunscreen and jumped back into the boats. Hannah and Jessie took the small one. The breeze had picked up. It calmed the scorching heat and drove the boats along.

"We should have brought fishing poles," Darius said.

Joe nodded. "Next time."

When they got to the other side of the lake, they pulled the boats to shore. Mo and Jessie waded back out in the water, while the others dug in the sand with sticks or just their hands.

"So, what's going on with you and Robert?" Mo asked Jessie. "I didn't know you liked him so much."

Once they were out far enough they needed to tread water, Jessie said, "I don't know if I like him *so* much. But I like him. He's cute."

"How did you end up kissing?"

"You saw it," Jessie said with a smile.

Mo looked over her shoulder. "Maybe not right now, but sometime, I want details!"

"Why should I give you any? You don't go into detail about you and Joe."

"We've been fighting for months. Besides, there's not that much to tell."

"Don't you like him as much as you used to?"

"I think I like him *more* than I let on, actually," Mo admitted.

"Well then, be prepared to share some details."

Hannah joined them and they swam closer to shore so they could touch the bottom. Mo wondered how could she explain to Jessie that even though she really, really liked Joe Parker, there wasn't anything physical to talk about. Sometimes it seemed that he wanted to kiss her, and she'd thought of it more than once, but it was a bigger step for her than it apparently was for Jessie, who was happy to kiss Robert because she liked him a little bit.

The temperature dropped a few degrees as the day went on. Joe sat next to Mo on the beach and buried her feet in the sand, halfway up her calves. Darius walked by and said, "That's one way to catch a girl."

Joe chuckled and smiled at Mo. "Then I wish I had done it weeks ago."

She wiggled her toes. "Ugh. I'm feeling trapped."

Joe helped her dig out. "I don't want you to feel trapped," he whispered.

She rose and walked down to the water to wash her feet. He followed. Then they made a sandcastle and moat in the wet sand. Joe's dark hair came forward as he leaned over it. It made him look boyish, but his strong shoulders reminded Mo that he wasn't the scrawny kid he used to be.

Robert plunked down in the sand beside them and turned his back so it was next to Joe's, then asked, "Whose sunburn is worse?"

"Oh, wow," Mo exclaimed. "You guys are going to be sore. I'd say it's a tie."

"Too bad you're not Asian," Darius said. "I'm sunburn proof."

Jessie shifted her bathing suit strap to show her tan line. "Native skin is great too. I hardly ever burn."

"Stop bragging!" Hannah said. "Redheads have the worst possible skin for summer sun."

Mo's shoulders were pink, but nothing compared to Joe's.

"Time to head back to town?" Darius said.

Hannah nodded. "I'm afraid so."

They all got in the large dinghy and paddled back across the lake, dragging the small one behind them. The breeze that had been at their backs on their way across the lake seemed stronger now that they were paddling into it. The friends took turns with the four oars until they reached their destination.

Mo and Hannah unscrewed the valves of the small dinghy and flattened it so it would fit in the trunk. Mo overheard Darius say to Jessie, "Mission accomplished." Robert and Joe picked up the little dinghy and carried it to Jessie's vehicle. Mo fiddled with the contents of her beach bag so she could listen to Jessie and Darius.

"I wasn't so sure it was working at first," Jessie admitted. "They had quite a discussion."

"And then their water fight broke out," Darius said, laughing.

"That was so funny," Jessie replied. "Good or bad? Good or bad?'"

"Yeah. But all's well that ends well, right? I'm glad you called. Robert and I have missed hanging out with you guys since those two started fighting. Well" —now Darius laughed— "I guess you can tell that Robert likes hanging out with you."

Mo looked over. Darius smirked.

Jessie shook her head. "See ya around," she said, picking up her beach bag.

Joe and Robert approached the girls as they walked toward the vehicles. Hannah fell into step next to Mo. She gave her a little smile as if she knew Mo had been listening to Jessie and Darius. "All's well?" Hannah asked.

"Yes."

When Mo got home she drank about a gallon of water, put aloe vera on her shoulders to cool the rosy burn, and checked her email. There was a letter from Bailey.

Tom was back for a visit. It's like he's a sailor with shore leave or something. He hardly unpacked his shaving kit, just plunked it on the bathroom counter. It was awkward being here with him, and I found places to be or stayed in my room most of the time. After he left, Laura seemed really sad. Things are kind of awkward between us too, like we both know there are things to say but don't know how to say them. Most of the time, Tom isn't an issue. It's almost as though he has simply disappeared and I have stepped into Brooke's life to fill the gap. Then things are perfect.

Bailey

Mo thought about the word *perfect*. She and Joe had made up, and it had been the perfect opportunity to kiss, but he hadn't even tried to kiss her.

25

Nathan's Mission Call

Nathan took the thick envelope in his hands and felt the weight of it. He lingered over the return address: The Church of Jesus Christ of Latter-day Saints. He laid the letter on the kitchen table, unopened, in front of his family.

"Why isn't Sarah here yet?" Jordy asked for the fifth time. From the chair next to his, Maury elbowed him.

Nathan bit the side of his lip. "She's on her way."

"We could open it without her," Jordy suggested. "We'll tell her where you're going as soon as she comes."

"We're all excited," Mom said from the head of the table.

"She wants to be here," Nathan said.

"We could act surprised."

Nathan just smiled and shook his head at his little brother.

"Then at least wait by the door so you can let her in right away," Jordy continued.

"The kid's got a point," Maury said. "Why don't you go man the door, Jordy?"

He bolted from the table and paced in front of the living room window. A moment later, he flung open the door. "Did you put on lipstick?" he said as Sarah approached the door. "You shouldn't take time for stuff like that. We've been waiting!"

"Jordy!" said Nathan, Maury, and Mom.

Seconds later, Sarah followed Jordy into the kitchen and slid into an open chair at the table. Nathan pulled the envelope toward him. "Are you ready for this?" he asked, looking at Sarah.

"I don't think so," she said.

"I am!" Jordy declared.

Mom held the telephone to her ear. "Laura, may I please speak to Bailey?" she asked in an icy tone. Mom's jaw was clenched but it relaxed when Bailey came on the line. "Yes, we're all here," Mom said. "Nathan's just about to open it." She set the phone on the table.

Nathan smiled and tore the end of the envelope off in one long strip. His fate for the next two years was inside this brown envelope. He pulled out the contents and picked up a single sheet of paper on top. "I should read it in order but—" He scanned through the letter with impatient eyes until he found the words. "I'm going to New York, New York!" he shouted.

Maury cheered and Jordy high-fived Nathan. Sarah clapped her hands and then hugged him and said congratulations.

Mom's hands were pressed together under her chin. A tear slid down her face. "That's so wonderful," she said, then came over and hugged Nathan tight. "And letters will get to you pretty fast. Slower than in Canada, but not too bad."

"We can probably email," Nathan said.

"Let me see the map," Jordy demanded.

Nathan turned the map that was included in the package so that it faced Jordy. "Here are the mission boundaries."

"Hmm. Which side of the United States is that on?"

"Come here." Nathan sat at the computer in the living room and pulled up a map of the United States on the Internet. "That's where I'm going," he said, pointing. He turned. Everyone, not just Jordy, was standing behind him.

Nathan would be a missionary. It was finally happening. All the time it took to get ready, all the money he had to save, all the preparation—now the goal was being realized. He went back in the kitchen and reread the letter on the table. "I have to be at the missionary training center in Provo, Utah, on August 8, 2001."

"Let's go out for ice cream," Mom said.

"I should try to lose my Canadian accent before I leave," Nathan said with a laugh as they got in the car.

"We don't have an accent," Maury put in.

"I'll cut down to one 'eh' a day," Nathan teased.

Sarah grinned. Then her gaze dropped and the smile fell from her face as she looked out the window. Nathan touched her arm and gave her a questioning look. She smiled again.

At the ice cream place, he ordered a sundae and then noticed a couple of guys he graduated with. While his family and Sarah waited for the treats, Nathan approached their table. "How's it going?" one of the guys asked him.

"I just got the news today—I'm going to be going on a Church mission to New York."

"Oh?" said one of them.

"How long?" asked the other.

"For two years," said Nathan. "I'm super excited."

"That's great. What will you be doing exactly?"

"Teaching about Jesus Christ, doing service . . . and I guess I'll find out the rest once I get there." He said the last part with a little laugh. Nathan asked the guys what they had been up to since graduation. He tried to focus on their answers, but all he could think about was his mission.

He joined his family at a table on the other side of the restaurant. A few minutes later President Harris and his wife came in. Nathan rose, and President Harris met him. "Is this a celebration?" asked the branch president.

"I got my call!" Nathan replied.

"Where are you going?" asked Sister Harris, her face lighting up.

"New York!"

"The city and the state have the same name," Jordy said.

President Harris shook Nathan's hand in a firm shake. "Congratulations. That's wonderful." Nathan had met with President Harris many times as he was preparing for his mission. The man was a spiritual giant.

They asked when he was leaving, and if there was anything he needed, and if he was going to miss his hair when he cut it shorter. Eventually, the Harrises went to order their food.

Mom looked at her watch. "We should get home and make the phone calls. Grandparents, aunts and uncles, and cousins all want to know where you'll be serving."

Back at the house, Sarah took Nathan's arm and said, "I should probably leave now. This is a time for you and your family."

"You don't have to go," Nathan replied. As he said the words there was pain mixed with the joy. He loved Sarah, even though he didn't say the words. But there was something so huge between them. They'd talked about spiritual things, and in many ways, they believed the same things. Still, she refused to set foot in the branch meetinghouse. She said she could be spiritual from anywhere; she didn't need a church.

"I should go," Sarah repeated.

Nathan opened the front door and walked her out to her car. "Will you write to me?" he asked.

"How can you even say that? Yes, of course."

"Do you promise? Not every few months but lots?"

"I'll write *back* to you lots."

"What do you mean?"

"As soon as I get a letter from you, I'll write you back." Her words were light but she swallowed and seemed to be holding something back.

Nathan touched her arm and said, "I'll miss you."

She nodded and pressed her lips together, then looked at the ground. "I'll miss you, too." Her voice was shaky.

"What is it?"

"It's all so real now. And you're going to want a Church girl when you get home, Nathan. You want to go to one of those temples."

He swallowed. Sarah didn't realize that he would be going to the temple before he left on his mission. To her, the temple was about marriage. They had talked about that once, and their date had ended soon afterward. He *did* want a Church girl. He just wanted *Sarah* to be that Church girl.

"Maybe it would be better . . ." she began.

It was as though a knife stabbed Nathan in the heart. *Maybe she's going to break up with me!* He blurted out, "I speak in church before I go on my mission."

She nodded. "You told me. The farewell."

"That's what they used to call them. But yeah, that's kind of what it is. I know what you said, but on that day—I'd really like you to be there."

Her hand trembled a bit as she brought it to her lips. "Okay, Nathan. I'll come to church that day." Her eyes looked glassy. She placed a gentle kiss on his lips and whispered, "I'll see you tomorrow."

A week later Nathan and Sarah were sharing an order of fries after working a shift at A&W. It had been a busy day. "At least it's cooler out here," he said. "I can actually feel the air conditioning."

"I think the grease sank into my skin," Sarah replied.

"I think my lungs are coated."

"It's summer! Don't people want fresh fruit in the summer? What's with all the fried foods?"

Nathan held up a fry. "What do you call this we're eating? And they do taste good. Do you know what I'm thinking?"

"Teen burger?"

"Yum, but no. I was thinking I don't know what your friend Carly looks like. Why have I never met my girlfriend's best friend?"

Sarah shifted on the other side of the bench. "I don't know. She's gone with her family a lot this summer."

"Not that much. It seems whenever there's a busy signal on your phone it's because you two are talking. What's Carly like?"

"You're starting to sound like my parents."

Nathan's eyebrows tightened. "Haven't they met Carly?"

"No."

"Why not?" It was obvious from Sarah's discomfort that there was something behind this.

"Because . . ." Her gaze was on the table for several seconds, and then she looked up with a determined expression. "Because she's not real."

"You have an imaginary friend?" Nathan gave her a sideways glance and finished the last two french fries. "Go on, explain," he urged when she didn't say more.

"She's not a figment of my imagination."

"I'm glad to hear that," Nathan said.

"But she's not exactly what my parents would consider an ideal best friend for me. You know by now that they are very rigid in their opinions, so I just don't give away too much about Carly. Are you okay with that? Can you trust me?"

"I can understand not introducing her to your parents. But why not me? What's wrong with her? Why are you so worried? You obviously like her; she is your best friend, right? Is she a drug dealer in her spare time?"

"Nothing like that," Sarah reassured.

"Then when can I meet her?"

"Never." Sarah slurped up the last of her root beer. "Well, maybe not *never*, but not yet. You're leaving on your mission, and I don't think it's a good thing to do before you go."

"Why not? Sarah, you're making me worry."

"Please, can we drop it, Nathan?"

"I don't want to drop it."

"I do. I don't know everything about you."

"I'm not hiding that my best friend is an axe murderer."

"Drop it."

He did.

The next few weeks flew by. Nathan was excited to serve his mission and couldn't wait to get started. At least that was ninety-eight percent true. The other two percent, he wanted life to slow down so he could savor his time with Sarah.

Soon it was time to pack for the MTC. Sarah had survived church on the day he spoke, but she seemed confused by the routine and whether or not Nathan was giving a farewell talk or everyone was there to say farewell to him. The meeting had been okay except that there was a lot of crying—Bailey, Maury, and especially Mom. Nathan tried to tell Sarah that church wasn't always so full of tears. The chapel had overflowed into the gym area. A lot of people had traveled to attend the farewell, and it was really nice to have their support.

At the end of the day, Nathan had asked Sarah, "So, what did you think?"

"Well, you certainly are sincere and your heart is in the right place with this mission. You want to share what is wonderful and good about your religion. I can't fault a guy for that."

He had been hoping she would feel the Spirit and have a real change of heart, but she said, "If only this religion didn't involve actually going to church."

He had laughed and said that of course going to church was part of church, but Sarah didn't seem to see the connection as clearly as he did.

Nathan had packed all morning and was almost done. Sarah was watering the flowers in her front flowerbed when he pulled his car up to her house. One last lunch date, and that would be it for the next two years. He'd be set apart that evening.

He got out of the car and walked toward her, his heart heavy. They'd have to say things this afternoon, important things he'd been avoiding.

She set the big yellow watering jug next to the front steps and met him. "All ready?"

He nodded. It seemed like a loaded question. He wasn't ready to leave her, but he was ready to serve the Lord. "Are you sure you want to go to A&W?" he asked. "For our last . . ."

"It's where we met," Sarah said. He opened her car door. "And it's where we had our first several dates before you were aware of it." They shared a smile. "It's the most romantic place in town."

"Yeah. You're right," Nathan said. He went around to the driver's side. He was in love with her. Completely. Totally. And he couldn't wait for this date to end.

When they entered the restaurant, his former coworkers met him with excited questions about his mission. They talked for several minutes before he and Sarah placed their order and while they were waiting for the food. One of the girls said, "Oh, poor Sarah. You're going to miss him."

"I definitely am."

One of the guys laughed and raised his eyebrows at her. "I can help with that."

A jolt like electricity shot through Nathan. It was jealousy and actual pain. And it was all the more sharp because of what he was planning to say to Sarah and what he was planning to *not* say to her today.

He took their tray of food to a table in the back. Sarah carried the drinks. Nathan devoured his hamburger but still felt empty inside. "Maybe you should take him up on his offer," he said with a nod toward the employees at the other end of the room.

"That was kind of awkward. Wasn't it?" Sarah laughed and shook her head. "I have no interest in taking him up on his offer."

"Two years is a long time. I don't know what's going to happen when I get back."

"Neither one of us knows that," agreed Sarah. She looked at the table then met his eyes. "Are you breaking up with me?"

"No. Not unless you want me to."

"Of course not."

"I just want you to know that I don't expect you to sit home alone every weekend. We don't know what the future will bring, and I don't want you to regret these years."

Nathan's heart beat like it was hammering its way out of his chest. "We are different in a lot of ways. In the long run, maybe . . ." His heart was breaking, and he couldn't finish the sentence. Couldn't make himself say, "Maybe we're not right for each other." He just stared at Sarah's beautiful, sad face.

"I know, Nathan," she said simply.

Then he said what he promised himself he wouldn't. "I love you, Sarah."

She reached across the table and laid her hand over his. He turned his hand and their fingers intertwined. "I love you too," she whispered.

26

Seeing Nathan Off on His Mission

The van was all packed in preparation for the trip to Edmonton, where Nathan would fly off to the Missionary Training Center in Provo, Utah. The stake president had been in the area the day before, so he set Nathan apart as a missionary. Earlier that day, Nathan had kissed Sarah goodbye and told her that they wouldn't be able to kiss after he was set apart. She had nodded but didn't seem happy about it.

"I told Sarah we'd pick her up," Nathan said as the family left the house.

His mom nodded. "She didn't seem comfortable at church the other day." Mom fiddled with her sweater, then took it off and slung it over her arm. "It would be nice if she started coming to meetings with us," she added tentatively.

"That would be more than nice," Nathan admitted.

Mom hugged him. "You look very handsome in your suit," she said as she pulled away.

Maury and Jordy were already in the car. Nathan and Mom got in. When they pulled up at Sarah's house, Nathan hopped out. Knocking on the door felt momentous. He wouldn't be doing this here for two whole years, but he would get plenty of knocking on doors. Sarah opened the door and started to lean in toward him. "Sarah," he said softly and held her forearms.

"Oh yeah," she said, then stepped over the threshold.

Her parents entered the foyer, and Sarah's mom called, "Goodbye."

"We wish you well," said Sarah's dad. It was plain they would be happy to see Nathan gone from their daughter's life.

"That's the warmest welcome I think I've received from them," he said as he and Sarah walked toward the van.

"Sorry about that," she said.

Nathan laughed. "They are pretty enthusiastic about goodbyes and documentaries."

"'Practical, factual, serious—that's what all your time should be spent on. Don't waste your time with fiction or fantasy.'"

"'Or religion,'" Nathan finished.

"They'd include that with the fiction."

"Too many people do." What Nathan really wanted to say, he kept to himself. 'What about you, Sarah? Where would you place spiritual things on the line between reality and fantasy?'

"Did you go for a run last night?" she asked, changing the subject. It was just as well.

"Yes, when it finally cooled off."

"You're going to get all flabby on your mission when you won't be able to run every night." Sarah's laugh was as beautiful as her shiny dark hair. Nathan would miss her laugh most of all. He wondered what would happen in two years—if her heart would soften about spiritual things, if her faith would grow. And if she would still be single after his mission.

Jordy rode shotgun next to Mom in the van. Nathan and Sarah took the second seat, and Maury lounged in the back. Bailey would be meeting them at the airport.

The countryside in August was beautiful. "I probably won't see many canola fields in New York," Nathan said as they passed a brilliantly yellow field. "I'll miss that."

"I know what I'll miss," Maury commented.

"What?"

"Your dating advice." Everyone laughed, and Maury added, "Without someone to remind me to date in groups, and not steady date, and who knows what else, I could make a lot of dating mistakes."

"I'll write it in a letter if I think of anything else." Nathan laughed.

"Oh, thanks!" Maury's tone was sarcastic.

"I'll miss your trusting heart," Mom said, looking at Nathan in the rearview mirror.

Nathan rolled his eyes. "Oh, Mom, not this story!"

"What? What happened?" Sarah said.

Maury cleared her throat. "An older neighbor kid, Kent, told Nathan he could learn to fly if he practiced hard enough."

"I was like five," Nathan put in.

"So Nathan would climb to the top of the fence," Mom said. "It was about four feet high, and he'd jump off and flap his arms really, really fast."

"It had to be fast enough." Nathan chuckled. "That's what Kent said in the flying lessons."

A burst of laughter came from Sarah. "Flying lessons?"

"You don't think a person could master a skill like that without lessons, do you?"

"And did your teacher ever demonstrate the actual flying?"

"No. We kind of skipped over that part. But I was sure I was falling slower all the time," Nathan said with a shrug.

Sarah giggled, but there was a strange gleam in her eye. "You had a great imagination, at one time. Then she whispered to Nathan, "I'm surprised it took you so long to imagine we were dating before you asked me out."

"Is that why you liked to watch *Peter Pan* all the time?" asked Nathan's mother.

He laughed. "I was so jealous of those Darling children! And I would have given anything for some pixie dust—you know, to speed up the learning curve."

Soon the airport was looming before them. Nathan was excited and apprehensive and thrilled and worried all rolled up in one emotion.

Mom pulled into a parking spot, and Nathan opened the sliding door and got his suitcases out of the back.

"That's it?" Sarah said. "It hardly seems enough for an extended vacation let alone a move."

"I'll take the big one," Jordy offered.

"That's okay," Nathan said.

"I want to carry it for you!"

"All right. Thanks, Jordy." As they walked side-by-side, Jordy asked Nathan, "Will you come to the airport when I go on my mission?"

"You bet."

Bailey came running the moment they entered the airport. She hugged Nathan fiercely and whispered, "I'm so proud of you."

"Are you sure you have everything?" Mom asked for at least the eighth time. "I wonder if it's too late for me to get a ticket."

"I can get myself to the MTC," said Nathan. "I'm a big boy."

"You're practically a baby," she whispered.

Nathan turned to Sarah. "I guess this is it. Thanks for coming. It means a lot to me."

"There's no way I'd miss out on spending two more hours with you." Her smile didn't reach her eyes.

Mom looked at her watch. "We got here a bit later than I thought we would, and they want you here two hours early for an international flight. Let's get in line. You check your luggage and get your boarding pass here."

Everyone got in line with Nathan and his baggage.

"Is this where I go through customs?" Nathan asked. He'd never been on a plane before, but he didn't want his nervousness to show.

"No it's on the other side," Sarah said. "There are signs."

Mom let out a big sigh. "I'll try not to worry about you at the other end."

"There will be other missionaries getting picked up at the airport. I'll be fine."

"You look so . . . missionary," Bailey said.

Nathan smiled. "Thanks. That's the idea. Oh, and tell Laura I said thanks for letting you borrow her car."

"Okay," Bailey said. "Although I would remember to thank her on my own."

"That's thanks from you. This is thanks from me."

Nathan spoke with the airline attendant and received his boarding pass. He turned and hugged each of his family members. Maury's and Bailey's tears ran in trickles, and Mom's were rivers. Jordy beamed as he hugged Nathan.

Sarah's eyes were dry. Nathan gave her a sisterly hug. "Goodbye, Nathan," she said. "I'll write."

He said, "I love you, guys," then he turned and walked into the next phase of his life.

27

Basketball Camp

"When's your basketball camp?" Tyrone asked.

"Tomorrow," Mo said into the phone. "I told you before that it was at the end of August."

"Right. Well, where are you staying? You could stay with my family, you know."

Right. That would be super awkward. "It's tomorrow, Tyrone," she said. "I've already made plans. I'm right in the dorms on U of A campus. I won't have a car—Mom's dropping me off. Besides, I could've stayed with Bailey. She said the bus route wouldn't be bad from her place but I had the money saved for the dorm and it's just easier."

"Could I take you out some night after you're done with the camp?"

"Sure. It runs from 9:00 until 4:00 every day. It would be great to have some plans occasionally."

"Occasionally—like every night?"

Mo laughed, not sure if he was serious or not. Joe had kept his promise to not act possessive or jealous, but he might not if she saw Tyrone every night next week. Still, lately Joe had seemed so nonchalant that she wondered if he even cared that much. *Poor guy—he just can't win. I'm mad if he's jealous, and I'm insecure if he's not.* "Bailey and I have plans one night," she said, finally answering Tyrone.

"Which night?"

"I can't remember if we decided for sure. I'll have to call her."

"Call me on Monday when you're finished with camp and let me know."

"Okay. We'll play it by ear."

On Monday afternoon, Mo was more tired than she ever remembered being in her life. Mom had insisted they leave at 6:00 that morning, which was good, because by the time they found the camp location, it was almost time for camp to start. There wasn't time to go to the dorm room, so Mo had two extra bags with her all day. After she finally got checked into her dorm, she talked to her roommate, a girl from Edmonton, for a few minutes, then showered and crawled into bed for a nap.

That nap had lasted three hours. Now it was 8:30, and she was starving.

Because her hair was wet when she went to bed, she pulled it back into a wild ponytail. Out in the living room, her roommate Becky was sprawled on the couch watching television. "You're alive," Becky said.

"Did you get something to eat?"

"Duh! Yeah!" Becky looked at her watch. "It's almost nine o'clock." She still had on the T-shirt she'd worn all day. She had been kind of lazy on the court, so maybe she didn't sweat that much.

"I hope the food court is still open," Mo said.

"I ordered a pizza. If you like pepperoni and olive you can have the other half." There was an open pizza box on the floor next to the sofa.

"Thanks."

"You can buy me dinner tomorrow," Becky said.

"Okay."

"We can go out somewhere. This place is a dump."

Mo nodded to be polite. Mo had budgeted her food money so it would last. Hopefully, Becky didn't think they were going someplace super nice. She picked the olives off a piece of pizza and sat in the chair next to the couch. A reality show was on TV. About every third word was beeped out.

"Those two are definitely going to get together." Becky pointed to the girl and guy on the screen. "They're hot for each other. It's totally obvious."

Mo dug her wallet out of her gym bag, took out some change, and went down the hall to the vending machine. When she returned, Becky was leaning forward and gesturing at the TV set. This was more energy than she showed getting back on defense. "I told you! Look at those two!" she said to Mo. The people in question were lying on the floor next to each other in a darkened room. They were whispering and it was hard to understand what they were saying, but there were subtitles.

"So he's cheating on somebody else?" Mo asked, sitting in the chair.

"With her!" Becky declared as if this was a personal victory.

"Hmm."

"I love this show. Don't you love this show?"

"I'm not into reality shows," Mo said. "I find them kind of boring."

"How could you be bored? Don't be stupid! This is great stuff."

Mo watched a little longer, but it wasn't getting any better. It was all petty disagreements and talking behind other people's backs. She rose from the chair.

"Where are you going?"

"I told someone I'd call him," Mo said. She didn't have a cell phone, but there was a regular phone in the dorm for making local calls. She got Tyrone's phone number from her wallet in her room and, knowing how much fun Becky was having spying on the TV couple, self-consciously dialed his number.

Tyrone's first words were "I was afraid you weren't going to call."

"It was a long day at the camp, " Mo said, trying to talk quietly so she wouldn't disturb Becky, "and I napped longer than I meant to when I got back to the dorm."

"Are you out of shape?"

"Apparently. I was exhausted. My roommate was nice enough to give me her leftover pizza." Becky turned her head and gave Mo a nod.

The phone conversation went on for several minutes, but since Becky could hear everything Mo said, she mostly let Tyrone talk. Eventually, he said, "So which day are you busy with your sister?"

"Oh, I haven't called her yet. But I guess tomorrow's out because I owe my roommate dinner."

"Wednesday, then?"

"Let's make it Thursday. I'll see Bailey Wednesday."

"And then you're gone on Friday. So much for my whole week's worth of dates! Will you at least call me on some of those other days, if you have time?"

Mo could almost hear the boyish grin in his voice. "You got it."

After she hung up with him, she dialed Bailey's number. A groggy voice answered the phone. "Bailey?" Mo said.

"Maury? Is something wrong? Is everyone okay?"

"Yeah. I'm at that basketball camp, remember?"

"Oh yeah. I worked the early shift at the restaurant. You woke me up. Scared me to death."

"Sorry."

"It's okay," Bailey murmured. "I'm usually in bed by 9:30. Call me tomorrow. Earlier."

The rest of the evening was spent watching mindless television shows, all of Becky's choosing. At one point as her roommate flipped through the stations, Mo saw a sitcom she liked and asked, "Want to watch that?"

Becky said, "That's lame," and then changed the channel. "This show is much better."

Mo wondered how Becky became the boss of the TV, and after she watched for a while she told Becky she was going to her room to read. But Mo might as well have stayed out there to watch because she couldn't concentrate on her book with the TV blaring through the thin walls.

At 11:00 she considered going to sleep, but the TV was still going in the other room. She turned off the light, then remembered her journal. She promised herself she'd start writing in a journal again, starting with this camp. She had gotten it as a gift last Christmas, and it didn't have a single word in it yet. Mo pulled the book and a pen out of her bag, sat cross-legged on the bed, and began.

I'm here at the basketball camp at the University of Alberta in Edmonton. My first day was mostly lay ups, dribbling, and passing drills. I'm dead tired even after having a long nap when I got back to the dorm where I'm staying.

My roommate has a strong personality and a weak layup. I miss Hannah and Jessie. I can't believe I have to take Becky for dinner tomorrow instead of going out with Tyrone. How did I get roped into that?

It feels weird to write in a journal again. The journal I kept before was burned in the fire and it's taken me a long time to want to start another one. I feel like I'm jumping in at the middle of a story and I don't want to go back and explain anything. And it's my journal so I don't have to.

If Becky doesn't turn down the TV, I'm going to scream.

Instead of screaming, she went into the next room and asked Becky to turn the volume down.

"We don't have to be there until nine o'clock," Becky replied. "You're not going to bed already, are you?"

"Yeah. It's almost midnight and I want to do my best tomorrow."

"It's just a camp not the provincial championship game."

"Still." Mo turned, and when Becky didn't adjust the volume she said, "Would you please turn it down? It's too loud for me to sleep."

Becky glared at her, snatched up the remote, and pushed a button until the chatter decreased a little. Just before Mo closed her door she heard Becky say, "Fun roommate."

The next morning Mo dragged herself out of bed. It had taken her close to three hours to fall asleep the night before. Between Becky's nasty comment and the volume of the TV, which she suspected was back at its original level, if not louder, it was impossible for Mo to sleep. The last time she looked at her watch it was 2:30, and she was awake for at least another twenty minutes after that. Now she stepped into the shower to help her wake up and to tame her bed-head hairdo.

Lunch was included in the price of the camp, but she needed to grab something for breakfast. The dorm room had a fridge, so she'd buy some milk and cereal for tomorrow. She didn't need to be eating out twice a day.

It was 8:25, and there wasn't a sound coming from Becky's room. Mo tapped on the door. Becky groaned. Mo opened the door slightly and said, "I'm leaving now."

"Who cares?" Becky snapped.

"Sorry. It's twenty-five after eight. Just thought I'd let you know."

"All right, Mom!"

Mo closed Becky's door and grabbed her wallet and gym bag. "Wow, and I thought she was grumpy at night," Mo whispered as she left the room.

Becky showed up at camp at 10:30, dumped her gym bag on the bleachers, and took out her basketball shoes. She kicked off her other shoes and sat on the floor, not in a hurry at all.

"You made it," said Mo when Becky finally grabbed a basketball from the rack and jogged up to where the other girls were doing a ball-handling drill. They were to bounce the ball in a figure eight around their legs. Mo was doing quite well with it.

Becky sneered at her. "I bet you like the standing drills. You run funny. Has anyone ever told you that?"

Mo didn't answer, but her ball hit her leg and she had to chase it down.

"Yeah, like that." Becky laughed. She imitated Mo, running as though she was skipping through a field full of daisies. Kelly, the girl next to Becky, snickered.

In the three-man weave, Becky overthrew the pass so Mo missed it. "I thought you were faster than that," she said loud enough for the camp directors and at least half of the other girls to hear. She was definitely going out of her way to make Mo look bad.

"We have time for a short scrimmage before lunch," said Terry, the head coach of the university boys' team.

"I hope Maury's not on my team," Becky said in a loud whisper.

"Me too," said Kelly, who'd been Becky's sidekick since she graced the camp with her presence this morning.

Mo tried not to let them get to her, but she was self-conscious when she was bringing the ball up the court. Becky and Kelly were mimicking her movements from the sidelines. If Mo took a shot and the ball didn't go in, she braced herself for their groans. It totally threw her off.

Soon Mo was so frustrated that she had to fight back tears. At lunch break, she called Tyrone and said, "Could you meet tonight? I've decided not to take my roommate out. I'll just pay for my half of the pizza I ate yesterday."

"Excellent idea! How soon will you be ready?"

"At 5:15," Mo said. "I don't want to be there a minute longer than that."

When camp ended, she hurried back to the dorm. She showered and put on a pair of jeans and a light-pink shirt. When Becky came in, Mo was adding just a touch of eye makeup.

Becky wasn't alone. Her snickering partner, Kelly, was with her. "Where are we going for dinner?" Becky asked Mo.

"You can go wherever you want. I left some money on the kitchen table for you."

Becky went to the kitchen table and picked up the note. "You weren't going to speak to me?" She laughed.

Kelly's laugh was sharp and loud.

"I wrote a note in case I missed you," Mo said. "I'm going out."

28

Dating Tyrone

The knock at the door was a welcome interruption. Mo strode
past Becky and Kelly and opened it.

"Hi Tyrone," she said.

He sauntered into the room. "How was your camp today?"

"Fine."

"Did you work hard?" His eyes took in the other two girls,
who were suddenly hovering nearby.

"It was a good day—skills-wise. We really worked on
defense. I'll get my purse and I'll be ready to go."

"Introduce us," Becky said.

"Hi," Tyrone said.

"I'm Becky and this is Kelly. We're in the same camp. And
it was a hard day, not a good day. Maury must be on something."
She giggled. "It would be really nice to get out of this place."

"We're stuck here," Kelly added.

"Except that Becky has a car," Mo said flatly.

Becky's gaze snapped back at Mo. "How do you know that?"

"Your keys on the table," Mo said. "Besides, you came with
your breakfast in an Arby's bag. Did you take the bus?"

Becky rolled her eyes. "Aren't you the little detective?" She
lowered her voice and said to Tyrone, "We're a lot more fun than

she is" —she jabbed her thumb in Mo's direction— "so give us a call. Do you have the number here?"

Tyrone's eyes were wide, but he nodded.

Mo pursed her lips and clenched her teeth. Why didn't he say something—something like "I've talked to you more than enough in the last two minutes to last a lifetime, thank you very much."

"Don't be too late," Becky told Mo in a sugary voice. "You need to get enough sleep for the camp tomorrow." Then she turned to Tyrone. "Bye, Tyrone. I hope we see you again."

"Yeah, bye," Kelly said.

Mo closed the door. After they walked a few steps, Tyrone said, "I think I almost had a triple date."

"What nerve."

He laughed. "It could've been something to talk about, though. I'd be a legend with the other guys."

"We could go back and get them if it's going to elevate your status," Mo said dryly.

"Yeah, right. I was just kidding."

They went to a Chinese food buffet, stayed for hours, eating and talking, then eating and talking some more. It felt good to vent about Becky and Kelly. Being with Tyrone, Mo could even laugh about it. He was sure Kelly and Becky were mostly jealous, but since he had never watched Mo play, she wasn't sure how much weight to place on the compliment. "So, you have her number," she said. "Are you going to give Becky a call sometime?"

Tyrone laughed. "I was so shocked, I didn't know what to say. Who tries to steal someone's date right in front of them?"

He needed to pick up some batteries for his video-game controller, so he and Mo stopped at a mall after dinner. They wandered around, window shopping and talking. When they came to the theater, they paused to look at the posters for the shows in the "Now Playing" section.

Back at Mo's dorm, when he dropped her off, Tyrone said, "I'd come in, but I'm afraid those girls might ambush me." His attitude didn't match his words. Mo was pretty sure he wasn't afraid. In fact, he seemed to like the attention.

"It could be entertaining to watch," Mo said, even though it hadn't been funny at the time. "I'd protect you. But I do want to get some sleep." She yawned.

"If she doesn't turn the TV down tonight, smack her."

"Hopefully she learned her lesson, since she was late for camp this morning."

"Hopefully," Tyrone agreed. "And are we on for Thursday? It's the last night for that chick flick you wanted to see."

"Chick flick? Don't you want to see that movie? We don't have to."

"It's fine. I just have to keep up a tough-guy image. Can't admit I actually want to see that show—I have to act like some girl is dragging me there kicking and screaming." Tyrone chuckled. "Call me if you get back from Bailey's early enough."

"Okay. Thanks for letting me vent."

"You're welcome. You hardly said much at all."

Becky proved she had not learned her lesson. She watched TV until after 3:00 in the morning. Kelly left at 1:00. Mo knew all this because she couldn't sleep with the combination of their talking and the TV.

At the end of the camp the next day, Mo was so exhausted she was almost in tears. She hadn't remembered plays, and her legs felt wobbly.

She went to the bleachers and sank down onto the bench where she had left her gym bag. Her whole body settled like sand slipping through an hourglass. She took off her basketball shoes and put on her regular sneakers. If she wanted to catch the bus to Bailey's, she'd have to go straight to the bus stop or end up waiting half an hour for the next bus.

A short time later, she was knocking at the apartment. Bailey opened the door, and the smell of whatever she was cooking wafted out. It was heavenly.

"What's the matter?" Bailey asked after looking at Mo for half a second.

"I've hardly slept."

"Come on in. Have a seat—I'm still cooking." Mo dropped her bag in the entranceway and collapsed onto the couch. The next thing she knew, Bailey was shaking her shoulder. "Sorry, I should have helped you cook," said Mo. "Didn't mean to fall asleep."

"Don't worry about it," Bailey said. They moved to the table, where a pan of lasagna and a big bowl of salad were waiting.

Mo told her about Becky while they ate.

"You have to stay here tonight," Bailey said. "You can sleep on the couch."

Mo nodded. "Okay, thanks."

After dinner, Laura and Brooke came home. Bailey read Brooke a story before bed. It was weird to be around Brooke and know that she was Bailey's baby.

That night Mo slept like a rock. It felt wonderful, and she woke rejuvenated even though she had to be out to catch the bus before 8:00. The morning traffic seemed to have a hopeful tone.

Walking in the gym with the other girls who were arriving, Mo felt like a completely different person from the day before. On the court, her reflexes were sharp and her mind quick. One of the instructors complimented her and even had her demonstrate a jump shot. When it was time for lunch, everyone gathered in the room off the gym where the food was laid out every day.

"Where are you from?" asked a girl named Meg who was behind Mo in the line for lunch.

"St. Paul."

"Where's that?"

"Northeast. It takes two hours to drive there," Mo replied. The two girls moved to the tables with their food and sat together.

Meg nodded. "I'm up from Lethbridge—my grandma lives here. I've been here for a month already. I'm staying in the dorm for this week. My roommate is that tall blond girl. She's pretty cool."

"Lucky," Mo said under her breath.

"Why do you say that?"

"My roommate stays up super late watching TV, and I can't sleep with the TV going. I asked her to turn it down, and now she hates me. She laughs at my mistakes— "

"Oh, that girl? Yeah, I couldn't believe she was so rude. That's it! This camp wasn't cheap, and I can tell you want to do your best. I'm finding you a new roommate or you can sleep on my couch. At least it would be quiet after midnight. Maybe that Kelly girl will switch."

Meg got up and went to the table where Kelly and Becky were eating. A few minutes later she returned and said, "Kelly doesn't want to move."

"Don't worry about it. It's not your problem."

Meg smiled. "Oh, but I'm on a mission, now." Meg moved from group to group and was in and out of the room with the food to talk with the girls who had moved to the bleachers.

If she was this determined to find Mo a better roommate, Mo could just imagine how driven she'd be in a basketball game.

Lunch break was almost over, and Mo didn't see Meg. Maybe she was in the bathroom. Mo made her way back into the gym. Becky approached her and stuck her bottom lip out in a huge pout. "Do you want to move out, Maury? Am I too mean?"

Mo started to say something about how they just like a different amount of sleep, but Becky and Kelly pretended to rub their eyes. "She picks shows I don't want to watch," Kelly said, mimicking Mo.

"And doesn't let me go to sleep at 8:00," Becky added. "I don't think she likes me. My feelings are so hurt."

"None of that's true," Mo said calmly. "But I think you need to learn a lesson."

"Oh, really? And what do you want to teach me?"

"That if you're rude and inconsiderate to people, you might end up alone." Suddenly, the gym was noticeably quieter, and Mo's words hung in the air as Becky's face fell.

Then Becky's expression morphed into a sneer. "You're the one who can't get along with people." Her tone lacked conviction, but she turned and stomped away with Kelly trailing behind her.

By the end of the day, Meg had found a girl whose roommate had canceled. Her name was Ronnie, and she was willing to let Mo move in. Right after camp got out for the day, Mo moved her things and took a shower. She phoned Tyrone to tell him about the new room, but no one answered.

At 6:00, she knocked on the door of her old room. From within, there were giggling and shushing noises. Finally, Tyrone answered the door. "I was early," he said, shrugging.

"And we couldn't remember which room you were in now," Kelly said. It was an obvious lie.

"Really?" Mo said sarcastically.

"I tried to get it out of them," Tyrone said.

Kelly laughed. "Oh, yeah, he tried everything."

"How should I know where you went when you ran away?" Becky said with a smirk.

Mo was already out the door.

"Good night, ladies," Tyrone said.

"Come again, Tyrone," Becky called.

"Having a good time?" Mo said when the door was closed.

"I thought you'd never rescue me," Tyrone said. He didn't seem at all distressed from his time with Becky and Kelly.

At the mall, Mo and Tyrone grabbed a burger at the food court and then made their way to the theatres. He linked arms with her. "You have to act like you're dragging me to this show, remember."

She smiled. "Right."

After the show, as they exited the building and headed toward the family vehicle Tyrone had driven, he asked Mo, "How did you like the movie?"

"Well, it was a little sappy. Some may even call it a chick flick . . ."

Tyrone grinned. "Who would call it that? Not me."

He walked her to the new dorm room, and she said, "Do you want to come in for a while?"

"Sure. I'd love to."

He stayed and talked to Ronnie and Mo for about half an hour. Then Ronnie declared that she was going to bed and reminded Mo to lock the door after Tyrone left.

"Good night, Ronnie," he said. The way he smiled at her — the way he smiled at all girls, including Kelly and Becky — was flirtatious in a not-so-subtle way. She didn't care if he flirted with other girls, but it didn't seem cool to do it while he and Mo were on a date.

Ronnie closed her bedroom door, and Mo and Tyrone were alone. "It's been great to spend time with you this week," he said.

"It *has* been good," Mo agreed, turning to see him better since he was sitting next to her on the couch.

"I really like being with you." He moved a little closer to her, his arm sliding along the back of the couch.

He was so close. There was electricity — or maybe anxiety — in the air. *Oh no, he is going to kiss me!* Mo jumped up and went to the fridge. There must be something in there to offer him, to distract him. She opened the fridge. "I forgot to move my food," she said. "I was going to offer you a drink."

Tyrone rose from the couch and met her in the kitchen. "Wild berry juice," he said, noting the jug of juice in there.

"I'm not going to take some without asking."

"Never mind. I don't need a drink."

Mo closed the fridge. When she turned, there was Tyrone. Inches from her face. "But you're very sweet to think of me," he said.

Her back was against the fridge. His eyes shut as his face moved closer. He was definitely going in for the lip meld.

"Uh, Tyrone . . ." she stammered.

"Mmm?"

He was still coming, so she reached up and intercepted his lips with her fingers. They were moist and partially puckered. His eyes flew open. "I'm sorry," she said. "It's just not feeling right yet."

"No? Oh, well, I should be going, anyway," Tyrone said.

"Okay. Yeah."

"It's been great seeing you."

"Yeah. You too."

29

Unspeakable Horror in New York City

Nathan went to sleep to the sounds of traffic and awoke to the sounds of traffic. He had grown to like it. New York City was everything he had hoped for. He and his companion, Elder Bennett, were teaching three families. One had three little girls. The oldest was nine, and they were always so excited to see the missionaries.

Nathan really wanted to visit the large publishing houses and agent offices in New York. He had saved all of his writing on three computer CDs that he kept in an inside zipper of his main suitcase. In a drawer back in St. Paul, he had three backup disks in "text only" format. He had made those copies to save him from predicted computer meltdown in the year 2000. The meltdown hadn't happened, and Nathan's computer was fine. Now the disks in his suitcase were turning out to be a big distraction. He wasn't on a mission to further his career, but maybe it wouldn't be so bad to print out a manuscript and drop it off while he was in the area. *When my mission is over,* Nathan thought, *I'll stick around and pound the pavement in a different way.*

Nate Mathews, his pen name for the newspaper, was close enough to his real name, Nathan Matheson, that at first he'd been afraid someone would figure it out. But no one had. He had submitted a column every month during his last year in high school, and after grad, he wrote them twice a month. The editor liked his work and was fine with the fact that Nathan didn't want a picture attached to his column. What he wasn't fine with was not getting another column for two years. Nathan had explained about his mission, but Mr. Duncan didn't understand why Nathan couldn't write a column during his downtime and send it by email. Nathan had written twelve extra columns before he left. Mr. Duncan agreed to run one every two months until Nathan returned, but made it clear that an extra column or two in his inbox wouldn't be unwelcome.

The Nate Mathews column was a humorous column for young adults. Sometimes the column was light, and sometimes it was more of a social commentary, but in a way that would make people smile as they examined their values. Occasionally, Nathan skipped the humor and had the guts to tell it like it is, something he believed should be done more often than not. His thoughts, his feelings—a very intimate part of him—were laid bare on the pages of the newspaper. And for now anyway, he didn't want anyone to know that he was Nate Mathews.

"Come on, Elder," he called to his companion on the other side of the room. "We hit the snooze button once already. Time to get up."

"What day is it?" mumbled Nathan's companion, a big, muscular guy.

"Tuesday, September 11th."

Nathan did 120 jumping jacks and then got a fresh towel for his shower.

"No sit-ups?" Elder Bennett muttered. "You're slacking this morning, Matheson."

"I feel . . . restless, like we need to get out of the apartment. Maybe there's someone we could meet on their morning commute."

"Maybe," Elder Bennett said, swinging his legs over the side of his bed.

When they left the apartment, Elder Bennett was carrying a bagel with cream cheese. "Our first appointment isn't until after lunch," he said.

Nathan was walking briskly. "Come on, Elder, finish your breakfast."

"I probably look like Elder Slob," Elder Bennett replied, brushing sesame seeds from his suit coat.

The New York skyline was a pleasant, familiar sight. But in the clear sky, a dark shape moved through the azure atmosphere near the buildings. It was an airplane. And it was getting far too close. The blood in Nathan's veins went cold.

"Elder?" he said, pointing at the plane as his stomach jumped into his throat. "It's too low. It won't—" In the next instant, the plane hit the North Tower of the World Trade Center. The airplane disappeared in a cloud of black smoke and orange flame.

Nathan's knees buckled. Elder Bennett dropped his bagel. It rolled three feet and settled cheese side down, but he didn't notice. Nathan gasped. "I've got to help!"

"You mean, *we've* got to help," Elder Bennett said.

Nathan slipped his backpack from his shoulders and stashed it behind a bush next to the front porch of a Victorian-style home. "We'll be faster without our packs."

"You're right." Elder Bennett shed his and put it with Nathan's. "Remember, house #603."

The missionaries ran through the streets toward the billowing smoke. "Do you think the pilot was drunk or something?" Nathan shouted.

"Or on drugs?" puffed Elder Bennett.

"Or just made a terrible error in judgment?"

Nathan soon outstripped his companion. Elder Bennett had been a football player in high school, but most of his athleticism was due to his size and agility, not speed. Nathan was frustrated with their pace but soon slowed. He should stay with his companion.

Less than twenty minutes later, an explosion echoed from above. Nathan and Elder Bennett stopped and cowered as their eyes were drawn up. They stumbled, trembling at the immense volume of the sounds of the collision. Elder Bennett shuddered. "Another one?" His hand covered his gaping mouth.

"It struck the South Tower of the World Trade Center. A second airplane." A chill crept over Nathan. "Could that be an accident?"

The elders' eyes turned from the billowing smoke and the true horror of what they were witnessing hit hard. This was not an error in judgment, an isolated incident of negligence, or even a random act of violence. This was an organized attack. "They need our help, Elder," Nathan told his companion.

"I can't keep up with you, Matheson. Just go!"

Nathan hesitated, and then an image came to his mind. A woman, in her late twenties, black, professional, crouching under something—a stairwell or a table somewhere.

He had to find her. He left Elder Bennett without another thought, praying as he ran. He didn't know where the woman was, or how he would find her. Or why she wasn't leaving the building.

Nathan neared the site of the wreckage. Crowds of survivors were covered in dirt and ash. Ash was everywhere. Black hair was white with it. Dark suit jackets were light gray. People were running for their lives, or staggering, or numbly putting one foot in front of the other.

Onlookers stood in small groups with terror on their faces. Wailing sounds came from every direction. People held tissues or sleeves to their mouths as they exited the two towers. Firefighters in bright gear rushed about.

Nathan's thoughts returned to the night of their house fire. Maury waking him. Running up from the basement together. The firefighters rushing past him only to find his father unconscious from the smoke. Nathan's body didn't want to breathe. The crowd seemed to tilt before his view. The black woman covered in white ash came forcefully to his mind again.

Nathan quickened his pace, weaving in and out of the people flooding from the World Trade Center and the surrounding area. *Careful, breathe,* he told himself as panic threatened. Blood dripped from a gash in a woman's arm. Two people helped someone whose legs were clearly broken. A man coughed into a bloody tissue. Injured people were everywhere, with pain and horror etched on their faces.

Sounds echoed in Nathan's brain—high-pitched screams, desperate moans, exclamations of shock, and repeated questions of why. As he reached the North Tower, a man was speaking into a cell phone. "Jenny! I'm okay, Jenny. Don't worry about me." Then the man's composure was gone and he wept without restraint. "I'm coming home."

Smoke was everywhere. Thick, choking smoke.

Nathan looked up and knew. The woman who needed him was in the North Tower. He couldn't run any longer, not because his strength was gone but because of the crowds of people exiting the building and flooding the stairways. He avoided their eyes and the raw emotions revealed there.

"Up!" a voice told him.

Nathan looked behind him, but no one was speaking in his ear. After the house fire, he had vowed to never ignore a prompting. So even though every instinct told him to run with the people exiting the building, he started up the stairs.

"Excuse me," he said after jostling a small man with watery eyes.

"Come on," said the man. "Nothing is worth going back for!"

Nathan ignored him and pushed through the crowd.

"Where do I stop?" Nathan prayed out loud. "Where will I find her?"

At the second floor, he paused. Nothing. He moved on. Third floor, fourth floor. Nothing, nothing. On the fifth floor, his heart burned stronger than his lungs. She was here. He crawled along the tile and followed his heart. "Don't hide!" he yelled. "I'm here to help you."

The office space was massive. Nathan crawled and crawled, stopping occasionally to cough into his sleeve. His white shirt had turned dark gray. Urgency drove him on. There wasn't much time. He called out, "Where are you?"

A faint voice answered his call. "I'm here. Help me."

Nathan turned at the sound. A woman matching the image in his mind was there. A filing cabinet had trapped her legs, and next to her was a picture in a cracked frame. He raced to her side and strained to lift the cabinet. She pulled her legs out and he lowered the cabinet. She crawled toward him and collapsed.

"Are you okay?" he said.

She didn't move. He leaned in closer, his blood pounding in his ears. He couldn't tell if she was breathing, but she had to be alive. He couldn't have freed her only for her to die. She needed to live more than Nathan did. There! Her chest moved, she was breathing.

Nathan crouched and got his arms under her. He lifted and held her against him, then turned and went back the way he'd come. A man's cries reached him. The words were mostly unintelligible, but it seemed he was mourning a friend who was dead and had to be left behind.

Nathan's strength was failing. He prayed for help as he joined the crowd exiting the building. He staggered down a flight of stairs. People rushed past him. His arms ached. His throat and lungs burned with the smoke. On and on he went. The stairs seemed to have multiplied. Darkness gathered at the edges of his vision.

Just as he reached the ground level, Nathan's knees buckled under him. He knelt on the floor with the woman still in his arms. A firefighter took her from him. She would make it! Nathan could leave this world now. Satisfaction wove through his being as though it was in the particles of smoke all around him.

Nathan fell forward on his hands and coughed as though his insides were coming up. Darkness filled his head as a sharp pain exploded in his side. A large man fell to the floor beside him, then managed to get back on his feet. The last thing Nathan saw before his world went completely dark was the man, a head above the crowd, leaving.

Three minutes later, at 10:28 AM, the North Tower of the World Trade Center collapsed.

30

Stunned at the News—and Lack Thereof

Mo and Jordy sat motionless in front of the television. It was 4:30 and they were watching what everyone had been talking about all day. The footage showed an airplane slamming into the South Tower of the World Trade Center, and then flames billowing out of the building. Survivors were emerging from the catastrophe, firemen were saving lives, and news announcers were trying to make sense of it all.

"What does 'hijacked' mean?" Jordy asked.

"I told you," Mo said. "It's when somebody takes over the plane."

"And they drive it?"

"Yeah," Mo replied, feeling hollow inside.

"Did they know how to drive it? Did it crash because they weren't good drivers?"

"That's not why they crashed."

"Then why?"

"They wanted to kill all those people, Jordy."

"But wouldn't the people driving the plane die too?"

"Yes." Mo's voice turned bitter. "It's too good for them! They deserve so much worse than an instant of pain before it was all over. Look what they've done to all these people." Tears streamed from her eyes. "And it was a moment of glory for them," she said angrily. "They were probably proud to do it. Some people are insane."

"You really mean they did it on purpose?"

Mo met Jordy's eyes. He was growing from a chubby-faced little child into a boy with a thin, wiry build, like Nathan. Jordy was seven years old, so something as terrible as this intentional mass destruction was difficult for him to understand. It was difficult for *anyone* to understand.

"Yes, they did it on purpose," Mo said.

The television showed the other attacks. American Flight 77 crashed into the Pentagon, collapsing a large section of the building. At the same time, another flight, United Flight 93, crashed into a wooded area of Pennsylvania.

"I hope Nathan wasn't there," Jordy said.

"There?" Mo pointed to the screen that showed the Pentagon, though she knew Jordy's thoughts were back at the New York site. "Nathan wouldn't be at the World Trade Center. All those people were going to their offices. There wouldn't be any missionary work going on there, especially at that time of the morning."

"Do you think Nathan knows what happened?"

"Of course." Mo sighed. Nathan could be walking underneath that smoke-filled sky. He could be among the people fleeing Manhattan on foot. But he was probably watching it all on TV, and Mo said as much to Jordy.

Jordy nodded. The phone rang, and he picked up the receiver. "Hello. Oh, hi, Sarah." There was a pause. "No, Nathan's a missionary. He was probably teaching someone about Jesus when it happened." A moment later, Jordy handed the phone to Mo. "She wants to talk to you."

As soon as Mo put the phone up to her ear, Sarah asked, "You really haven't heard from Nathan?"

"No. I don't think we will. Missionaries are only allowed to call home on Christmas and Mother's Day. But in an emergency like this . . . well, I don't think they'll wait for P-day to tell us they're okay."

"Well, please just let me know when you hear from Nathan. Or about him."

"Of course, Sarah."

Mom got back from Edmonton a few minutes later. She joined Mo and Jordy on the couch and put an arm around each of them. "I'm so sorry I had to be at the office today," she said. "That you had to see this alone." Mom nodded toward the news show, which was once again playing footage of the airplanes hitting the towers. "I called Nathan's mission president as soon as I heard."

"Oh, good!" Mo said. "What did he say?"

"He promised to phone when he knew Nathan was safe."

"When was that?" Mo asked.

"Six and a half hours ago." Mom seemed to give herself a mental shake. "He'll call soon."

She doesn't want us to worry. The thought made Mo more anxious.

"They are away from their apartment, which is natural for a missionary," Mom explained, "and they might have a dinner appointment tonight. Church members are always having the missionaries over for dinner. If they are at a dinner appointment, we might not hear about him until tonight." Mom got up and paced. "I'm sure he's fine. Bailey was at school when it happened." Mom glanced at the TV. "It's so horrible."

"You talked to Bailey?" Mo said.

"I caught her at the restaurant ten minutes before her shift. There was static on my cell. She seemed far away."

The TV showed images of New Yorkers running from the falling debris. Some firemen and fire trucks were unable to reach the scene because of the wreckage in the streets. "It began as a peaceful Tuesday morning," Mom said. "All those people just going to work. And now this!"

The reaction of world leaders was the next order on the television agenda. Mom looked at her watch, then picked up the phone and ordered pizza.

Pizza was Jordy's favorite. "Thanks, Mom," he said when she hung up the phone. Then seemingly out of the blue he added, "Nathan's probably watching it on TV."

Mom nodded at him with a pained expression on her face, then left the room, her shoulders shaking under her thin, patterned top. She hurried into the bathroom and closed the door behind her. Mom's muffled sobs brought tears to Mo's eyes. *Where is Nathan?*

At 9:35 PM the phone rang. Mom snatched it up. "Oh, President Jensen!" She huffed like she'd been holding her breath. "Thank heavens, you've finally heard from him."

Mo and Jordy hovered next to Mom.

Mom gasped. "What do you mean you can't find him? Was he—was he at the World Trade Center?"

Mom listened and then dropped the phone from her ear as though lifting it was too heavy a burden. It hung at the tips of her fingers. Mo scooped it up before it fell. "Hello, hello. Is my brother okay?"

"I wish I knew more," President Jensen said. "He and his companion were separated this morning. Elder Bennett searched for him most of the day before he finally contacted me."

Mo held the phone away from her ear and switched it to speakerphone. "Where could he be?" she asked.

"I'm so sorry," replied President Jensen. "We just don't know yet. After it happened, he and Elder Bennett were running to the Twin Towers to try to help. Elder Matheson outran his companion. That was the last Elder Bennett saw of him today. I know how worried you must be. But Elder Matheson is very responsible, and I'm sure we'll hear from him soon. I'll phone the moment we know more."

"Thank you, please call." Mom choked out the words. "Any time of the night is fine."

"Yes, of course," President Jensen said before hanging up.

A few minutes later, Mo answered a knock at the door. There stood President and Sister Harris. "We just heard from Nathan's mission president," President Harris said.

"We didn't think you should be alone," Sister Harris added, stepping forward.

Mom fell into the woman's shoulder. "He can't have him," Mom cried. "Not my husband and my son! The Lord wouldn't do that to me, would He?"

"We don't know anything yet," President Harris said, "so let's not assume the worst. He's probably fine."

Mom shook her head. "He would have phoned if he was okay. Nathan wouldn't let people worry. He would think to call."

"Maybe he can't get to a phone," Sister Harris suggested.

"No, he'd find a way."

The telephone rang. Mom jumped up and grabbed the receiver. "Yes?"

She handed the phone to Mo. "I can't talk."

"Hello?" Mo said into the phone.

"It's Sarah. Have you—"

"No, we haven't heard from him. His mission president called. He's not sure where Nathan is." Sarah gasped. "He's going to call when he knows. I'll call you when we hear anything."

"Okay. The moment you do—"

"Yes, I promise."

The rest of the evening there was little talk, many tears, and nonstop TV news coverage that replayed the events of the day. The Mathesons searched the footage for a tall, thin missionary. President and Sister Harris stayed until it was time for bed.

31

Strange Sights by the Light of the Moon

Mo sat on the corner of her bed and opened her photo album. These were the first pictures taken after the fire—the youngest any of her siblings would look in pictures. That wasn't quite true. Aunts and uncles had given her mother some photos with their family from pre-fire days. They were mostly from a family reunion held when Mo was five. There were seven pictures in all. Mom had those pictures tucked away somewhere in her bedroom. Most were so blurry that they were more depressing than comforting.

Mo turned the page of her album. Here was a shot of her dribbling a basketball, with Nathan guarding her. Another picture was of Nathan sitting cross-legged on the trampoline. Jordy jumped beside him trying to "crack the egg." Nathan and Mo were playing foosball in another shot. Her favorite was a recent photo Mom had taken of Nathan, Bailey, and Mo on their way to an etiquette dinner at the church meetinghouse. Nathan wore a suit, and Bailey and Mo were in dresses. It was after Bailey had the baby. Nathan's smile dominated the picture, but his eyes were serious—almost sad. There was always a mix of emotions in Mo's older brother since the fire.

Where could he be? Why had he gone to the World Trade Center? He was just one person. What did he think he could do?

Mo knew she would never fall asleep, not for a long time, anyway. She slipped a sweatshirt over her t-shirt and went to the front door. "Where are you going?" asked Mom, sitting in the darkened living room.

"Can't sleep," Mo said. "I'm going for a walk. I won't go far."

Mom nodded and whispered, "Okay."

Mo put on her shoes and walked out into the cool night air. She walked around the bend in their subdivision, past the park, and made her way to the center of town. Businesses were long closed, and homes were mostly dark. She passed Sarah's house. Sarah loved Nathan — Mo was sure of that. Whether or not Nathan loved her back was in question, as far as Mo could tell. She had never seen anyone so uncomfortable at church as Sarah was on the day of Nathan's farewell. And he would never be really happy with someone who didn't share his faith.

A television on in the living room was the only sign of life at Sarah's house. She went to the door and was about to knock quietly when she saw through the half-open curtain that it wasn't Sarah who sat in the recliner, but an older woman. Sarah must have gone to bed.

Mo started for home. She wove through the streets when suddenly she spotted Sarah's car, or one just like it, though there weren't many BMWs in St. Paul. It had to be Sarah's parents' car.

Mo paced the block where the car was parked. She shrugged and moved toward home twice, but as she reached the end of the block she couldn't do it. Mo peeked inside the vehicle. Under the streetlight it was clear that this car was spotlessly clean, something Sarah had joked about around Mo. She said her dad had vehicles you could eat off of but never eat in. There was a purse on the passenger-side floor that looked just like Sarah's. Two other cars were parked in front of this house. Maybe there was a party going on. No, Sarah wouldn't be at a party the night of her boyfriend's disappearance. But Mo couldn't think of a reason Sarah would be at someone's house so late at night. She should be at home, waiting for a call from Mo or Mom about Nathan.

Mo turned and walked, again determined to head for home, but then she heard a door open and turned. It was the house where Sarah's car was parked. And there was Sarah in the doorframe. Someone stood behind her in the light from the house. He was about five inches taller than Sarah and had broad shoulders. Suddenly, they embraced. Mo gasped. It was a long hug, and the guy whispered something in Sarah's ear. She touched his face with her open palm before she left.

Mo ducked behind an evergreen tree while Sarah got into the BMW and drove away.

32

What's Your Name, Cowboy?

Nathan tried to focus. There was a billowing sail of a ship in front of him. Or the padding inside a coffin. Or the clouds of heaven? The sharp ache in his head was back. Then there was movement next to the shining rod that reached toward the sky, soft words he didn't understand, and then he was lost again. The shining rod turned sideways in his mind, and he dreamed of the Lehi's vision in the Book of Mormon, about the tree of life. He was one of those people trying to reach the tree with the most brilliant white fruit—the fruit that would make him happy, the fruit that was the love of God. He clung to the iron rod that led to the tree.

Clouds again. A metallic sound accompanied their movement. Which seemed wrong. Someone was next to him. He struggled to open his eyes. It was a woman, and she smiled. There were deep lines around her mouth, and her plump cheeks reminded him of apricots. "Glad to have you back with us, cowboy," she said. Her voice was young, as if it had forgotten to age with the rest of her.

"Where's the woman . . . the black woman in a business suit?" Nathan mumbled.

"You asked about her before," the woman replied. "I'm sure she's fine. You just relax."

"Is she okay?"

She started to repeat her assurances but then stopped and said, "Tell me her name. She might be here in this hospital. Names don't always help, though. You haven't told us your own name yet, cowboy."

"Name?"

She gave him a soothing pat on his arm. Now he realized that the white clouds were the curtain around his bed. The iron rod that stretched heavenward was an IV stand. He was in a hospital.

"Going to tell me your name today?" asked the woman.

"Today? Isn't it Tuesday, September 11th?"

"That was yesterday."

"My name?" Nathan's eyes were closing. He reached up to the area where his nametag hooked into his shirt pocket, but both the tag and his shirt were gone. The clouds and the iron rod were gone. He was drifting. "Elder Matheson," he said, but he wasn't sure he said it out loud.

33

A Long-Awaited Phone Call

The next day just after 4:30 in the afternoon, the phone rang. Sitting on the couch, Mom jumped about six inches into the air and snatched up the phone. "President Jensen?" she exclaimed almost before she had the phone at her ear. She listened then said, "Hospital?"

Mo sped to her side, hoping to hear the voice from New York through the phone. "Oh." Mom's exhale was forceful. She turned to Mo. "He's okay—he's going to be okay."

Jordy moved around Mo. She hadn't realized he was behind her. She ran to Mom's bedroom and got on the other phone.

The voice of Nathan's mission president echoed slightly. "They don't want us to use the cell phone for long in the hospital, so we'll have to make this quick. Here he is."

"Hi, Mom."

"Nathan! Are you okay?"

"Hi," Jordy yelled. And Mo called out a hello.

"Hi, everyone." Nathan's voice was weak. "Sorry I made you worry."

"Oh, Nathan, it's so good to hear your voice!" Mom said. "What happened?"

"I saw the planes. I saw it happen. I went into the North Tower."

Mom gasped. "What were you doing there?"

"It was after the planes hit. Someone needed my help."

"There were firefighters for that."

"I had to help too."

"Oh, heavens! You're not trained, and you don't have the protective gear. And it would destroy me if I were to lose you now—"

"You were just like the firemen!" Jordy interrupted.

"I had to go inside, Mom," Nathan said calmly. "There was a lady I knew I needed to find. I felt it." He paused, and when he began again his voice was scratchy. "It was the strongest prompting of my life. I saw an image, a vision, of the woman who needed me." He paused again. "For months before my mission, I had felt there was something I would have to do—something strenuous."

"Did you find her?" Mo asked.

"I did. And I can only hope she made it the rest of the way out. I could see the door when I collapsed. I was carrying her."

Mo frowned. "The rest of the way . . ."

"You risked your life—" Mom said.

"And you don't even know if she made it?" Mo added.

"No, I don't know. I've been trying to follow every prompting, every signal, trying to make up for . . ." Nathan paused for several seconds, and Mo thought the call had been disconnected. She jumped slightly when her brother said, "Mom, Maury, Jordy, I'm so sorry. This has been eating at me, and it's going to keep eating at me if I don't admit this to you." There was a sniffling noise as if he was crying, which was strange because Nathan never cried. He was always the strong one. "There's something, uh, something I have to tell you. Our fire, in St. Paul." Now Nathan was definitely crying. "It was my fault."

"Oh, Nathan, no. No, it wasn't," Mom said. "It was the wiring."

"But I heard the alarm. I was the first one to hear the alarm, and I pulled a pillow over my head to block out the irritating noise. I'm so sorry. We could have gotten out sooner. Dad might have—"

"You can't think like that," Mom quickly cut Nathan off. "Dad made a choice. It was his choice. I blamed myself for quite a while, thinking I could have kept him from going back into the bedrooms. I should've insisted he stay with the rest of us. But we can't think like that, Nathan. We have to forgive ourselves, and forgive Dad."

Nathan let out a moan. "I could have done so much better. I was awful." His breathing was loud. "I've tried to make up for it," he choked out. "Tried to step into Dad's shoes. I'm so, so sorry."

"Please don't blame yourself, honey," Mom said. "I love you. We all love you."

"Of course we do," Mo said, but her mind was flipping through the "what ifs." When she had gone into Nathan's room the night of the fire, his pillow was over his head. She hadn't thought much about it, but obviously his inaction had been haunting him all this time.

"I better go," he said.

"But Nathan—"

"I'm okay, Mom. Maury and Jordy, please forgive me. I love you guys." With that, the line went dead.

Mo was overcome with conflicting emotions—relief that Nathan was okay, anger that he had ignored the alarm, pride that he went into the World Trade Center to save someone, and sadness that Dad wasn't there to be proud of him, too.

She walked out of the bedroom. Her mother was on the phone with Bailey, passing on the good news, and then calling other family members. When Mom finished, Mo picked up the phone and dialed Sarah's number. Mo didn't want to call, after what she'd seen the other night in front of that guy's house, but she would feel guilty if she didn't let Sarah know that Nathan was okay.

Sarah's voice was breathless when she answered. "Hello! You've heard something."

"Nathan has been found," Mo said. "He's in the hospital but is going to be okay."

"Oh, I knew it!" gushed Sarah. "I've been so worried, but I kept telling myself that he is doing this mission for God, so God would save him. I know that's not necessarily the way things work, and that sometimes bad things happen to good people, but oh, I'm so glad this wasn't one of those times!"

Sarah went on for another thirty seconds, but all Mo could think was *You obviously moved on fast.*

34

P-Day Splits

One week later, Nathan was back in his missionary apartment with a stir-crazy companion. Elder Bennett paced the small apartment like it was a cage at the zoo. Suddenly, he stopped and asked, "Do you want some juice?"

Reclined on the couch and propped up with pillows, Nathan was writing on a legal notepad on his lap. "I'm fine," he said.

"I hate to leave you behind."

Nathan looked up and smiled. "Good one, Elder. Honesty is part of the thirteenth Article of Faith, you know. 'We believe in being honest, true, chaste, benevolent' —"

"What?"

"I'm not blaming you," Nathan said gently. "If I was stuck here with a sick companion, I'd be jumping at the chance to go to the mall too."

"I'll bring back some candy or something for you."

"Thanks. How did you get Elder Pack to agree to trade places for the day?"

Elder Bennett shrugged.

"Come on."

A smirk spread across Elder Bennett's face. "You know how he's always after my favorite tie."

"Yeah."

"And seriously, I could have any tie I wanted, or all his ties, for my Japanese one."

"Or a sacrificed P-day?"

"I said he could have it until one of us gets transferred out of this area, and then he has to return it."

"So, basically, he's renting your tie?" Nathan laughed, but a pain shot through his head so he stopped. He sank lower into the pillows on the couch and closed his eyes.

"You better put that neck brace on," Elder Bennett ordered, then strode into the next room and returned with the brace. He helped Nathan fit it into place and adjusted the pillows.

"You didn't know you came on a mission to be a nurse, did you?" Nathan said with some bitterness. "And I sure as heck didn't know I'd be useless."

"That lady you saved wouldn't feel that way about you, Matheson."

"I can't stop thinking about her. So many people were killed, and they needed saving as much as she did. Why was I supposed to save her? Could I have done more?"

"You did all you could possibly do. You kept going until you collapsed. Maybe she's going to be the next President of the United States."

"God doesn't love presidents more than He loves you and me, Elder." Nathan was thoughtful for a moment. "But maybe she'll help put some important laws or political policies into place that will affect thousands of people." He was quiet again, this time because his temples were throbbing. When the pain subsided he continued, "I saw her so clearly, Elder."

Elder Bennett sat in the chair and rested his elbows on his knees. "She was your mission, Matheson. If you do nothing else while you're here, you'll know you did what you were sent here to do."

"I'm not going home."

"I know. You'll get better."

There was a knock at the door, and two elders entered the apartment. Elder Pack was a round-faced guy with small eyes. Elder Jenkins towered over him.

"Well?" Elder Pack rubbed his hands together.

"It's in my closet," Elder Bennett said, then led the way.

"How's the sicko?" Elder Jenkins asked.

"Hanging in there," Nathan replied.

"You look like you've been run over by a truck."

"You're sure full of compliments," Elder Bennett said as he entered the room again.

"Well, he does."

Nathan touched the stitches holding together the gash on his forehead. He must look like Frankenstein's monster. The doctor suspected that a kick to the head had split open Nathan's forehead, given him a concussion, and caused the neck trouble. He also had abrasions on one side of his face, as if his cheek had been dragged across the sidewalk.

Nathan coughed hard, and the tissue he held to his mouth came away with black-tinged phlegm on it.

"Gross," Elder Pack said.

"Sorry. I tried to hide it. Between the house fire we had before my mission and 9/11, I probably have the lungs of a pack-a-day smoker."

Elder Pack put on the black tie decorated with red Japanese characters. "This is so cool."

"Well, Elder Bennett, are you ready to finally get out of this apartment?" said Elder Jenkins. He looked at Elder Pack. "Enjoy your P-day," he added with a smirk.

Elder Bennett said, "I'll get groceries. We won't be that long."

"I have lots of letters to write," Elder Pack said. "I haven't written to my parents in three weeks."

"Pretty slack," Nathan said. The missionaries were supposed to write home every week. At least Elder Pack would be busy writing and not wasting Nathan's time with a lot of conversation. Nathan did more writing than just to his family on P-days. The events of

9/11 had changed the world, including his family. In a letter, Mom had explained how difficult it was for Jordy to understand what had happened. Childhood innocence had taken a big blow that day. That was the theme of the piece Nathan was working on now.

Elder Pack blabbed on for several minutes about a girlfriend back home. Then he opened his wallet and handed a picture to Nathan. It was the third time Nathan had seen it. He nodded and passed it back to the elder.

"We went out most of senior year," Elder Pack said.

"I thought it was all of high school."

"Uh, no. Junior and senior year."

The details seemed to shift around a bit, depending on the day, and Nathan had started to wonder if Elder Pack really had a girlfriend.

Nathan looked down at his writing pad. Elder Pack took the hint and started on the promised letters home.

Sweet—Nathan could concentrate again.

Within the hour, there was another knock. Elder Pack looked over at Nathan as though hoping he would jump up to answer the door, but Nathan only glared at him. Elder Pack set his paper on the coffee table and went to the door.

President Jensen entered the room, and Elder Pack stood a little straighter. "How are you feeling, Elder Matheson?" asked the mission president.

"Okay."

"Here's the list of your next doctor's appointments." He handed Nathan a note written in block letters. "I'll pick you up half an hour before those times. Don't look so glum. You are improving more quickly than I expected. I'm sure you'll be back to full-time missionary work before you know it."

"I hope you're right."

"I was a doctor before I retired. A darn good podiatrist." President Jensen grinned, but when Elder Pack only stared, the president explained, "That's a foot doctor."

Nathan smiled. "I don't have bunions. My problems originate at the other end of the body."

"That's a nice tie, Elder Pack." President Jensen pointed to the tie draped around the missionary's neck. "New trade?"

"Yeah. Isn't it cool?" Elder Pack went to the hall mirror to admire it.

"What are you writing, Nathan?"

Nathan glanced over at Elder Pack, then said in a low voice. "I told you about the articles I wrote before my mission."

"You said the newspaper had enough columns to tide them over until your return."

Nathan nodded. "Yes, but they wanted more, so I spend a little time writing on P-days."

"May I?"

Nathan handed the note pad to his mission president and watched the older man's face as he read. President Jensen's expression was somber. When he finished reading he softly said, "Would you like me to fax this to the newspaper in Canada? Or we could type it for you and email it."

"President?"

"Let's not make a habit of it. But this is timely."

Nathan slowly got off the couch. He hung on for a moment until he was steady and then went to his room and returned with the information.

"And your family doesn't know you do this?"

"Do what?" Elder Pack said.

Nathan shook his head and sat on the couch. "Nothing." He looked at Elder Pack. "You should bring out the box of cookies and we'll have a few."

Elder Pack went to the kitchen.

"I'm sure Sister Jensen wouldn't mind typing it up for you," President Jensen told Nathan. "She's very fast, and I'll email it tonight."

"Thank you." Nathan shook hands with his mission president. "Oh, and sign it Nate Mathews," whispered Nathan.

"I'll let myself out," President Jensen said. "I certainly don't need cookies," he added with a hand on his stomach.

When he was gone, Elder Pack said, "What a browner. After the AP job?"

"For your information, I wouldn't want to be assistant to the president." Nathan took a chocolate-chip cookie out of the box Elder Pack handed to him. "I'd much rather be meeting and teaching people. I'm going crazy not being able to go to our appointments. I have to talk to other missionaries to find out how our investigators are doing." Nathan's head was aching again, so he said, "I need to lie down."

"Go ahead," said Elder Pack. "I'll write my parents another letter so I won't have to do one next week."

"That's really thoughtful of you," Nathan mumbled.

35

Jessie's Advice

During her free period, Mo went to the school library and sat at a table in the back. Her schoolwork was a virtual mountain this year. When she finished one assignment there was always another one looming ahead.

She tried to focus on a page in her Biology 20 textbook, but other images filled her mind. Images of 9/11, which is what the news shows kept calling it. Terrorism was something she hardly thought of before September 11th, but now she thought about it almost constantly. Nathan had been there, right inside the North Tower of the World Trade Center.

Tremors of sympathy vibrated through Mo. He must be haunted a thousand times more than she was. He'd been there in the wreckage, among the panicking people and the smoke and flames. It must have brought back the horrible day of his family's house fire.

For the third time, Mo read the same paragraph from the textbook. The library door opened, and Joe and Jessie walked in. Mo closed her book. They sat at her right, and though she acknowledged what they said, her thoughts were back with Nathan under that sky of violence.

After a few minutes, the librarian strode over and said, "I suggest you find another spot to socialize."

Mo gave an apologetic shrug. The other librarian was much nicer than this one. This lady seemed to think if she wasn't listening for noise infractions, she wasn't doing her job.

"I didn't hear the bell for lunch," Mo told Joe and Jessie as the three friends walked out of the library.

"It didn't ring. We got out of math early," Joe said.

"We already told you that, Mo," Jessie added.

"Oh. I guess I was thinking about Nathan and didn't hear you."

"How's he doing?" Jessie asked.

"Pretty good. Last I heard, his doctor still didn't want him to do anything strenuous, though."

Joe shook his head. "I can't believe he was right there in one of the Twin Towers."

They stopped at their lockers. The lunch bell went off, and soon Hannah joined the three friends.

"Hey, Joe, where are your buddies?" Jessie asked as they made their way to the lunchroom.

"If you mean Robert, I think he's home sick today."

"I wasn't being specific," Jessie said defensively. "I haven't seen Darius yet today, either."

"Just tell us, what's with you and Robert?" Joe nudged Jessie with his elbow. "We all saw you guys kissing in the dinghy."

"One kiss, not kissing." Jessie was scowling.

Joe raised his eyebrows. "Kissing that lasted long enough for all of us to see you through the binoculars. Robert's pretty shy, you know. If you like him, you'll have to let him know."

"Thanks for the advice," Jessie said. "But . . . I don't care." She pointed at Darius in the far corner. He waved them over to a long table where he was sitting. "I could give you some advice," Jessie said to Joe. "If you want to let Maury know you like her, maybe you should kiss her."

Mo looked away, pretending she hadn't heard.

Hannah and Mo walked ahead of Joe and Jessie.

"Well, I, uh . . ." Joe stuttered. He lowered his voice and Mo barely heard him say, "Do you think she wants me to kiss her?"

"You guys have been going out for so long."

"Not that long."

"Long enough," Jessie said.

"And she's been dating other guys."

"Only Tyrone, and only over the summer."

Hannah and Mo slid into the bench across from Darius, while Jessie and Joe hung back.

"Has Tyrone" —Joe hesitated— "kissed Mo?"

"Yes," Jessie's tone was challenging.

Mo's jaw dropped. *I can't believe she would say that! She knows he tried to kiss me but that I didn't let him. . .*

"All right, he hasn't kissed her either," Jessie finally admitted.

"So, why did you say he did?"

"I thought it might get you moving. Somebody needs to light a fire under you boys."

Joe frowned. "That wasn't very nice."

"Maybe not," Jessie said.

Mo opened her chocolate-covered granola bar and took a bite, trying not to smile.

36

Missionary Work Green Light

"So I have the green light?" Nathan asked.

The doctor, a competent young woman, nodded. "I wouldn't suggest running a marathon anytime soon, or helping someone move, but walking and resuming your regular missionary work shouldn't be a problem."

Nathan jumped off the examination table, clutched her hand, and shook it firmly. "Thank you very much, Doctor."

The next morning as Nathan was eating breakfast with his companion, Elder Bennett said, "Maybe I should rush you out of the house while you're still eating your bagel."

"That was inspiration," Nathan replied. "I would never have hurried you if it hadn't been really important."

"Yes, yes, you're a very thoughtful guy. Now eat your breakfast."

"The Ryans are going to be baptized next Saturday. If we have time, I'd love to visit them today."

"We should be baptizing them," Elder Bennett complained. "We knocked on their door, we started teaching them, we challenged them to be baptized."

"At least we get to be there for the baptism. Besides, they must have gotten close to Elder Pack and Elder Jenkins the past couple of weeks, and that's why they asked them to perform the baptisms."

"I suppose."

Nathan and Elder Bennett spent the day knocking on doors, and they were able to teach at two houses. About seven o'clock they made their way to visit the Ryans. Maycie, the angelic-looking nine-year-old, answered the door and said, "Are you all better, Elder Matheson?"

"Yes-siree," Nathan replied. "Are your mom and dad home?"

"Dad is," she said, then turned and yelled, "Dad, the nice missionaries are at the door!"

"Come on in," said Mr. Ryan from the couch in the living room. "That's how the kids refer to you two, 'the *nice* missionaries.' They missed you."

Maycie returned with her younger brother and sister. John, the six-year-old, jumped into Elder Bennett's arms and declared, "I thought she was lying. It's always those other missionaries that come." The way John said "other" made it sound as if he didn't like the other elders as well.

"This is my friend Ben." John motioned to a boy hanging back a few feet, staring at the two missionaries. "He's listened to some of the discussions too."

"Very cool," Nathan said. "Nice to meet you, Ben." The boy seemed familiar.

"Elder Matheson couldn't come to teach us because he was still hurt from helping people when the towers were hit," Maycie told Ben.

"We went to one of your churches that's close to our house two times," Ben said.

"Ben's not old enough to get baptized, but his mom said he could talk with you guys."

"We missionary guys?" Elder Bennett said, swinging John over his shoulder.

John squealed and laughed.

"Can't I get baptized on Saturday, too?" Ben said. There was a hopeful look in his eyes.

"I'm so glad you feel like you want to be baptized," Nathan said. "When you turn eight years old, you'll be able to take that very important step."

Maycie shuffled her feet and told Elder Bennett, "I wish you could baptize me, instead of one of the other guys."

"We didn't really build the same kind of friendships with the other elders," Mr. Ryan explained. "But that's not the important thing, right, Maycie?"

"I know," she said, pouting a little. "I want to get baptized, no matter who does it."

"We'd all prefer one of you two," whispered Mr. Ryan.

"You can have whoever you want to baptize you," Nathan replied. "Anyone who holds the priesthood and—"

"Really? I didn't think there was an option? Would you . . . " Getting choked up, Mr. Ryan extended his hand to Nathan.

"I'd be honored."

"Can I have Elder Bennett then?" Maycie asked with a toss of her blond curls.

"Of course," Elder Bennett said.

Maycie grinned. "Just wait till Mom finds out."

Fifteen minutes later, Nathan and his companion left the Ryans' home.

"Just wait till Elder Pack finds out," Elder Bennett said as he and Nathan walked down the sidewalk.

"That wasn't our fault," Nathan said.

"They're going to think we swooped down and took their baptism."

"Let them think what they want. It's not *their* baptism, anyway."

Elder Bennett laughed. "It sure isn't."

37

A Terrible Example

Mo finished her shift at McDonald's and pulled out her car keys—well, Nathan's car keys. Though Bailey really wanted a car, she didn't trust herself with his car in the city, so Mo was using it.

"Can I bum a ride?" Garrett asked, bounding up to her.

"Sure."

They walked to the vehicle and he tapped out a tune on the roof of the car while he waited for her to unlock it. "Going to the football game tomorrow?" he asked as they buckled their seat belts.

"Nah."

"Come on, you and me under the bleachers. It could be cozy."

Mo gave him half a smile and drove to his house. "See you later," she said after she parked the car at the curb.

"Give it some thought. I'll bring everything you need." Garrett raised his eyebrows at her and then got out of the car.

As she drove, she thought about what she needed. She definitely didn't need Garrett to flirt with her. Basketball season was around the corner, and she needed more endurance on the basketball court, and hang time in her jump shot. And yeah, a good guy would be okay too. Jessie figured Joe should kiss her. Yeah, that would be okay, too.

Mo checked her email when she got home from work. There was a message from Bailey.

Dear Maury,

Brooke is such a sweetheart. Tonight I played patty cake with her and read her stories. She has her favorite books and wants me to read them over and over again. She fell asleep during the last book, and I just sat there smoothing her hair away from her perfect little face.

I'm going to tell you something—something you can't tell anyone. I know I can trust you, Maury. You've always been there for me. I feel okay most of the time. But sometimes, when I'm not studying or watching TV, when my mind is free to wander, I feel this vague sort of discontent. I don't know what it is or why I'm feeling it. It seems to pounce out on me when my guard is down. When the apartment is quiet, when I'm on the bus, it's like it's hiding in the shadows until it finds an opportunity to jump.

And now I think I've finally figured it out. I hate Tom. He's going to ruin everything. It's going to hurt so bad when he is back for good and I'm out of the picture. It's almost a feeling of panic. Mom would probably say she's not surprised. She didn't want me to move in with Laura and Brooke. Well, I don't think I can possibly endure having to leave.

When Tom's back, there will be no evenings of block-building, no mornings of stories and rhymes. There's even a good chance that Laura and Tom will move away. Then what about me? I don't regret giving Brooke up for adoption. It's not that. I am definitely not ready to be a mom. But now that I've been living here, things are getting strange and muddled. I don't want to be Brooke's mom, but it's like she's my sister and she's going to be taken away from me. Can I go back to getting a picture in the mail now and then? I know that's all I wanted, but now I'm in deep. I'm part of Brooke's life. I'm caught—trapped, in a way.

I can't let it happen. I can't sit back and let the course of events I see coming tear my heart apart. I'm going to have to make things happen. I have to get rid of Tom. Laura is still under his spell right now, but that's going to change. I have time and I'm going to use it.

I need to go. Talk to you again soon.

Bailey

Mo reread the line "I have time and I'm going to use it." What in the world did Bailey mean? A feeling of dread settled on Mo's shoulders.

This was too important to answer via email.

Bailey couldn't afford a cell phone, so Mo picked up the phone and dialed Laura's home phone.

On the second ring, Bailey answered with a soft hello.

"What did that email mean?" Mo said without returning her sister's greeting.

"Maury? Hi. It means what it said."

"What are you planning?"

"I'm not going to tell you the details—I don't even know all the details. But I will tell you this, Tom doesn't deserve to be in Brooke's life."

"You're scaring me a bit," Mo said, and that was an understatement.

Bailey's voice dropped to a whisper. "Laura's just getting home. I better go." Bailey hung up.

The next day at school, a girl Mo worked with at McDonald's asked her to take her shift so the girl could go to the football game that night. It was a good excuse to give Garrett, and Mo might as well get in as many shifts as possible before basketball season.

Just before her shift ended that night, she went into the dining room to wipe down tables. Sarah's BMW was pulling into the A&W lot across the street. Someone was with her, and they walked into the restaurant. Sarah's someone was tall and broad-shouldered. Nathan had barely escaped death, and here was Sarah with a boyfriend. Maybe this was the same guy she was hugging the other night, or maybe she had a whole line of guys she was dating. Either way, Nathan deserved to know.

Mo finished her shift and drove across the street, then entered the restaurant. Sarah and the guy were sitting at a booth and seemed in the middle of a deep conversation. Mo hesitated at the A&W entrance for only a second and then strode right up to their table.

"Hi, Maury," Sarah said with a guilty smile.

"Hello," Mo said, taking in the guy's features. He had gorgeous eyes and looked like a model you'd see in a magazine under the heading "Keys to Flirting With Him." He was super cute but the exact opposite of her brother. Nathan was lean and this guy was muscular. Nathan had dark hair and this guy was blond. Nathan often had a serious look on his face, and this guy didn't seem to have a care in the world. The biggest difference was that Nathan was gone and this guy was here.

Mo crossed her arms. "Are you going to introduce me?" she asked, still standing at the head of their table. She had decided this was definitely the guy from the other night.

Sarah seemed frozen in place. When she didn't say anything, Mo continued, "Well, I thought your new boyfriend might like to know that you haven't broken up with your old boyfriend yet—at least not that I've heard." It suddenly occurred to Mo that maybe Sarah had written Nathan a "Dear John" letter as soon as he got out on his mission. Maybe they really had broken up. If so, Sarah's concern when he was missing was just a girl being concerned about her ex-boyfriend.

"He's just a friend," Sarah said finally.

"Really?" Mo rolled her eyes. Not only had she seen Sarah hug this guy at his house, now that Mo saw him up close, she knew that Sarah would be attracted to him. Any girl would be. "So you and Nathan didn't break up?"

"Of course not," Sarah replied.

"Then what's going on?"

Sarah had that deer-in-the-headlights look. The silence seemed to last forever, but it was probably only about ten seconds. "No, never mind," Mo said. "I know you're just going to lie." Sarah started to protest, but Mo cut her off. She stared into Sarah's eyes for a moment before she said, "Nathan deserves to know."

Sarah jumped to her feet. "Don't tell Nathan, Maury. We're just eating fries— we're not doing anything wrong."

"You're allowed to 'eat fries' with whoever you want. Does Nathan know you're going out with someone else?"

"It's not like that . . ."

"Look, go out with whoever you want. Just don't let Nathan believe you are still in love with him when you're not. Don't you think it would hurt more when he finds out you're dating other guys behind his back? I'm not saying you have to wait for him. I'm not so sure you guys are right for each other anyway. I've wanted to tell Nathan that but I thought it wasn't my business. I'm glad you have a new boyfriend. Have six for all I care. But Nathan deserves to know you're not sitting home alone waiting for his letters. He deserves the truth."

The guy piped up then. "Well, you don't know the truth, so you're not the one to tell Nathan anything."

"What do you know about Nathan?" Mo asked. "And an even better question is what does Nathan know about you?"

Turning to Sarah and her pleading, guilty eyes, Mo said, "Have you mentioned this 'friend' to Nathan?"

Sarah shook her head.

"That's what I figured," Mo said. Then she turned and hurried out of the restaurant.

Once she was outside, she turned to watch them through the window. The guy stood and put his hand on Sarah's shoulder.

Sarah covered his hand with hers. She looked sad as they spoke.

They were definitely a couple, and if Sarah was lying about it, they were probably a serious couple. Mo got in the car and drove out of the parking lot. When she came to the streetlight, she turned left. Joe would know what to do.

Sister Parker answered the door. She was a stout woman with cheeks that looked like she was hiding a crab apple in each side. "Maureen? Well, hello. I didn't know you were coming over."

"Joe doesn't know either," she said. "Is he home?"

"Go on into the living room. I think Joe's in his room."

Mo said hello to Brother Parker and Joe's brother Mark, who were watching a program on TV. Brother Parker asked about Nathan and said how relieved he was that Nathan was recovered. Mark echoed what his dad said and then got distracted by the TV. Brother Parker left the room.

"Hey," Joe said as he entered the room. He looked like he had just wet a comb and run it through his hair. He was wearing a black sweater with stripes of gray and blue down the sleeves. He looked wonderful. "What's up?"

Mark glared at them and turned the TV up louder.

"It's nice outside." Mo nodded toward the door. They put on their shoes.

"Don't you have a jacket?" Joe asked.

"I forgot it at work," she said.

He grabbed a couple of jackets out of the front closet and handed one to Mo. "Here. Mark's is smaller than mine."

"Thanks." They walked into the crisp night and started down the block. "I think Sarah is cheating on Nathan," Mo said.

Joe wrinkled his forehead. "Really?"

"Yeah. I've seen them together twice. I actually saw them hugging the other night, and tonight I saw them at A&W. I talked to her, and she definitely looked guilty. She said they were just friends but he was cute and I can't believe it. Joe, what should I do?"

"He hasn't even been gone that long," Joe said. They walked in silence for a bit, and then Joe asked, "Do you want to be the one to tell him?"

"It would break his heart. He gave me a hard time about dating decisions, and I know he had to be kind of conflicted about Sarah not coming to church and stuff. But he liked her so much."

"She came to church sometimes, didn't she?" Joe said.

"Just on Nathan's last Sunday. I don't think she even believes in God, Joe. Nathan wouldn't want me going out with someone who's not even Christian. He gave me an earful over Garrett."

"Well, Garrett's scum." Joe looked sideways at Mo and smirked.

"Yeah, I guess." She laughed. "He's really not that bad. But anyway, Nathan fell hard for Sarah even though he knows it will never work out between them. Their beliefs and values are too different. It's doomed and he still—"

"If it's doomed, why do you have to do anything?"

"I don't know what their agreement was when Nathan left. I can't see him asking her to wait for him when there are so many things that will keep them apart when he comes back, but doesn't he deserves to know what's going on? Besides, it might help him get over her, and then it won't hurt so bad later."

"I suppose finding out would bring a quick end to it," Joe said. "And it might actually be easier than breaking up over beliefs, in the long run."

"It's even worse if he doesn't."

"Doesn't what?"

"Break it off. If he compromises his goal for a temple marriage because he's in love with Sarah, he'll come to regret it. There's always the chance someone will come around, that their faith will grow and that they'll accept the gospel, but you never really know how someone's heart is going to change over the years. I'm afraid for him, Joe."

"Nathan wouldn't do that, Mo."

"Remember Sister Andrews . . . Carol. She did. Love makes people do things, rationalize things." The chill of the wind stung Mo's cheeks. "I should tell him that Sarah's cheating on him. He'll be sad for a while and then move on." Mo said it with conviction but then wavered. "Don't you think?"

Joe shrugged. "It's a tough call, but you make a good case."

She smiled.

Joe glanced at her sideways again. "You look good in that jacket."

"It's way too long in the arms." Mo shook them over her hands. "When did Mark get so big?"

Joe started to say something but then stopped. He cleared his throat and started again. "Maybe they really are just friends, Mo. Sarah and that guy. It's a possibility."

"Not a very good possibility! I saw them hugging and he was—"

"Really cute."

"Don't tease me, Joe."

"What about you and me? We were friends for a long time, and I think you're really cute."

Though the compliment was not lost on her, Mo said, "Exactly. We *were* friends."

Joe laughed. "Oh, right. We're not a very good example. In fact, we're a terrible example." Joe turned and faced her. "You're more than cute. You're beautiful and you're my best friend. I'm so crazy about you I can hardly stand it sometimes." His arms came around her shoulders, and he gently pulled her closer. Mo's hands settled on his back. "We're a terrible example," Joe repeated.

"And I think it's about to get worse," Mo said.

They smiled at each other, and time seemed to hover at that one moment. It felt right to be in Joe's arms. When Tyrone wanted to kiss her, she was so nervous and just wanted to get away. Now she was content, safe, and happy. But she might have stopped breathing.

Their lips touched ever so gently, and then Joe's mouth moved with hers into a full kiss. In that kiss were all the things Mo and Joe had ever been to each other—basketball opponents playing one on one, youth partners working side by side laying sod, very first dates, partners in misunderstandings and reconciliations, forever friends, and more in love than she had ever admitted, even to herself. When they pulled apart, Mo could still feel the sensation and had to look at his lips to be sure Joe wasn't still kissing her.

He hugged her, and she rested her forehead next to his jaw. She never wanted to move from this spot under the streetlight on 47th Ave. The town could come along and put a fence around them so people walking along the sidewalk wouldn't collide with them. Mo wouldn't mind. It was a long time before Joe released her.

"It's getting cold," he said as he took her hand. They began walking back the way they'd come.

"I hadn't noticed," Mo replied. With Joe's smooth hand around hers, she couldn't imagine ever being cold or lonely again.

"Will you tell Nathan about Sarah?" Joe asked.

Mo shook her head. "He's been through enough." If Nathan felt half of what she was feeling right now, she couldn't be the one to end it.

"Sarah might do it herself if she thinks you're going to tell him."

"That would be best."

Joe opened the front door of his house. "Want to watch some TV?"

"No. I bet Mom is wondering where I am. She knew I was off work at 8:00."

"You could call her."

Mo looked at her watch. "All right. For a little while." She had homework to do, but it could wait an hour. There was no way she'd be able to concentrate on math right now anyway. Joe was holding her hand.

38

The FedEx Letter

Elder Bennett paced the small apartment like a lumbering grizzly. "The suspense is killing me, Matheson. It isn't every day that a missionary receives a letter by FedEx."

Nathan looked up from the paper in his hands. "What do you think it is?"

"I don't know. Is it a Dear John letter—a fast Dear John letter?" Elder Bennett started to smile but then must have summoned his compassion. "You're a good guy, Elder, and you've only been out on your mission for a couple of months. What kind of cold-hearted girl would dump you so soon, and in such an expedited fashion?"

Nathan looked at the pages again. He had read the long letter twice, some parts three times, and hadn't uttered a word.

Elder Bennett went out to the kitchen and came back eating a sandwich. He sat next to Nathan and asked, "Well, Elder, what did Sarah say?" When Nathan didn't answer, Elder Bennett placed a consoling hand on his companion's shoulder. "Sorry, buddy! But if it isn't meant to be, it isn't meant to be. Try to look on the bright side. You'll be able to really focus on your mission without a girlfriend back home."

"That's not it," Nathan muttered.

"What?"

"Just listen and tell me what you think."

Nathan turned to the first page of Sarah's letter and began to read:

Dear Nathan,

Hi, how are things with you? I hope this letter reaches you before you hear from Maury. She loves you and I know she'll tell you everything, but please believe me, she doesn't really know what she's talking about.

Elder Bennett interrupted. "What did Maury say to you?"

"Nothing. I haven't gotten a letter from her in a couple of weeks," Nathan said. Then he continued reading:

I don't know where to start. I guess the most logical place is with Carly. There is a reason you've never met her, and it's not that she doesn't exist. She does exist, but she's not a girl. Carly is how I refer to my best friend, Charlie.

You saw Charlie a couple of times when he came to A&W to talk to me. You asked who he was, and I told you he was just a friend. You probably don't remember, but I was worried that you thought there was something between him and me.

I've known Charlie for a long time. We did go out for a week or so, but it was obvious there would only be friendship between us. My parents saw this tall, handsome guy hanging around their daughter all the time and assumed we were dating. They didn't trust us to be alone together, and they thought we were getting too serious

about each other. Nothing I said made any difference.
Then one night everything blew up. Charlie and his dad
had a big fight, so Charlie came over. My parents had
already gone to bed. I let Charlie sleep in my room that
night, on the floor. The next morning he tried to sneak
out, but my dad caught him. I won't go into the whole
awful scene that followed. I'm sure you can imagine.

My parents saw this as proof that I had been lying to
them all along. They ordered me to never see Charlie
again. For months they hardly let me out of their sight.
It was so unfair, Nathan. Charlie and I were best friends,
with no romantic relationship at all, and my own parents
wouldn't believe me.

I saw Charlie at school and it made me miss him. I had
girlfriends, but the whole unfairness of the situation made
me kind of rebellious, I guess. Why were my parents telling
me who I could and couldn't be friends with? Why were they
ruining something as precious as true friendship? I guess
everything is black and white with my parents. There is no
room for gray or exceptions to rules—there is no room for
anything that doesn't fit with their view of the world.

I've told you that my parents are always watching
documentaries. They don't believe in things that can't be
verified. They don't believe in make-believe. They don't
believe in fairy tales. I didn't hear the story of Snow White
until I was in kindergarten. If the story had a moral, my
parents would tell it. I heard The Three Little Pigs because
it teaches lessons—be prepared, don't be a slacker, there
are bad guys in the world who will take advantage of you
if you are. Did I ever tell you that I'm not allowed to read
anything that's not factual? Novels that are assigned for

school are the only exception. My parents don't approve of those either, but because they are part of the curriculum they don't have much of a choice. Other kids complain about reading assigned novels; I eat up those novels.

I didn't write to you to whine about my parents. I'm only telling you because I think it may help you understand my relationship with Charlie. My parents couldn't accept our friendship, and I refused to be manipulated into giving it up.

So I invented Carly. "Carly" and I mostly just talk on the phone. There is an element of risk in seeing each other face to face. When you and I started going out, my Carly lies were already so engrained it just seemed easier to go along with it than to set you straight. Besides, I didn't know how you would react to the idea of your girlfriend having a guy for her best friend. Even now I am completely agitated wondering if you believe I can have a good-looking guy for a best friend and not be romantically interested in him.

Maury saw us together tonight. It must not have been the first time. I've never seen her like that. She thinks I'm cheating on you, Nathan, and even though you never asked me and I never promised not to go out with other guys while you're gone, I want you to know that I haven't. Charlie is my friend.

I hope you are completely recovered now and can go on with the work that I know you love. I'm sorry to distract you with these things now.

Love,
Sarah

Nathan folded the letter and slipped it back into the envelope.

Elder Bennett smiled. "It's a lot better than a Dear John, even if I only understood about half of it. Carly and Charlie are the same person?"

"Apparently."

"What's the matter? Don't you believe her? Do you think something is going on with this Charlie guy?"

"No. I'm sure Sarah is telling the truth."

"Then why do you look so depressed?"

"She didn't trust me with the truth before. And if it weren't for the confrontation with Maury, she'd still be lying to me today."

39

Round 2 with Becky

Mo and Joe climbed up the bleachers and sat with Jessie, Darius, and Robert. Hannah was warming up with the rest of the girls' volleyball team. They were undefeated so far this year and were expected to do well in the tournament that day. "Has anyone seen this Edmonton team play before?" Darius asked, nodding toward the opponents, who were also warming up.

"Hannah told me they've lost two of their league games but they're probably playing a lot tougher teams than in our league," Jessie said.

"Don't you wish you were still playing volleyball?" Robert asked Mo.

She shrugged. "I liked volleyball but I'm too far behind to start playing again." She looked at Joe. "Maybe if I hadn't turned into a basketball maniac in junior high, I'd still be playing."

"Do you miss it?" asked Joe.

Mo smiled. "Not really. I have basketball."

"Do you know that girl?" Darius said to Mo.

"What girl?"

"On the other team. The one at the back of the line. She was just pointing this way."

"Oh, that's my roommate from that basketball camp at U of A."

Jessie gasped. "Your nightmare roommate?"

"She's pretty," Robert mumbled.

"I forbid you to like her," Mo said.

"I bet Jessie does too," Darius said, elbowing Robert in the ribs.

For a while, it seemed no one knew what to say. Jessie tossed her bangs out of her eyes and stared at the volleyballs sailing over the net while Hannah and her teammates practiced serving. Robert left, saying he was going to go get a drink. The rest of the group stared at Jessie.

"Will you guys stop it?" she said.

"Why don't you go talk to him?" Joe suggested.

"Talk to who?"

"He wants to talk to you."

"We're together all the time," Jessie said. "He's had plenty of opportunities to talk to me. And we do talk. You guys should mind your own business."

"Like you did last summer?" Mo said. "I seem to recall quite a lot of butting into my business."

"That was different. You and Joe just needed a good nudge."

"I'm going to nudge you out to the snack bar right now," Mo said. She stood and grabbed Jessie's arm.

"This is ridiculous. I have nothing to say to him," she said but allowed Mo to prod her along. "He's checking out other girls right in front of me. This is stupid."

Robert was at the front of a crowd surrounding the snack bar tables. Mo and Jessie hung back.

"You guys all think I'm in love or something because of one kiss," whispered Jessie. "A kiss can mean a lot of different things. It was just a kiss. It was a nice summer day, we were in a matchmaking kind of mood after bringing you and Joe together, Robert said he thought I was pretty, and we kissed. That's it."

"Do you like him?" Mo asked.

Jessie shrugged, and Mo didn't blame her. Robert had kissed Jessie and then never singled her out again in all the times they had been together as a group.

"He's shy, you know," Mo said.

"I know. But he has a telephone at his house. No! Look, it doesn't matter. I don't care."

"Here he comes."

Robert stopped in front of the girls and offered them candy from his bag of M&M's. Mo was closest to him, but she stepped aside. Jessie took the candy. "You guys wait here for me," Mo said. "I think I'll get a drink too." She walked over and got in line at the snack bar. When she returned, Robert was shuffling from foot to foot and neither he nor Jessie was saying a word.

"You couldn't walk into the gym by yourself?" Jessie said.

"Is it too late in the year for dinghies?" Mo surveyed her friends. "You two could make good use of one."

Robert turned red. Jessie glared at Mo and said, "Let's go."

Before they were halfway to the bleachers, a volleyball came flying and hit Mo in the side of the head, knocking her off balance. It was like a missile to the temple. She fell and hit her head on the hardwood. She blacked out for a second, then sat up with her elbows on her knees and her head resting in her hands.

"Are you okay?" It was Jessie's voice. Robert's hand was on Mo's back, supporting her. Suddenly, Joe stood in front of her.

"I'm okay," she whispered.

Becky stood smugly in front of Mo, bouncing the volleyball like she was dribbling a basketball. "Hey, sorry about that," she called, though her expression showed anything but sorrow.

The whistle's signal gathered both teams to their benches, and Mo and her friends returned to their seats. The right side of her face stung. "Is it red?" she asked, turning her face toward Jessie.

"Yeah."

"I bet there are lines from the volleyball."

Jessie gave her half a smile. "Nope, no lines."

"No wonder you switched rooms," Joe said.

"Yeah, I thought you were being a big baby," Darius added.

Mo huffed. "Oh really? Thanks."

The Edmonton team beat the hometown girls in the first set 25–19. The second set was an even worse loss, with a final score of 25–10. After the game, Hannah joined her friends in the bleachers.

"You guys played well. They were a tough team," Mo said.

"Rough and tough," Joe agreed. "Did you see what happened to Mo?" There was fury behind his eyes.

Hannah shook her head.

"Number 8 is Becky, Mo's roommate from basketball camp," Jessie said. "She threw a ball at her head before the game started."

Hannah turned and scanned the gym behind her. "Really? She's insane. Who holds a grudge like that?"

"And lashes out like that," Joe said between clenched teeth.

His anger in Mo's behalf made a little warm knot in her stomach. She grabbed his arm and rubbed the inside of his elbow with her thumb. Becky was rude and mean, but Mo wasn't really hurt.

The group of friends climbed down the bleachers and moved out to the hallway. "Do you think we have enough time before the next game go to the Dairy Queen?" Mo said.

"Hmm," Hannah said.

Becky strutted toward them and stopped, so full of attitude it rolled off her in waves. "I hope we meet up for basketball, too," she said. "Your coordination looked a little off today." The girl with her giggled.

"That's one perspective," Robert said.

"What's your name?" Becky asked.

Jessie piped up, "His name is Robert, and he thinks you're cute."

"I don't either," Robert said.

"Go ahead and admit it," Jessie said. "Maybe you could have a relationship that actually went someplace if you did."

Becky took a step toward Robert, and he took a matching step backward. "Maybe we should go someplace and talk about this alone," she said.

"No thanks."

"Don't be shy. We'll get away from all these extra people." Her hand was on his arm now.

Robert looked flustered. "I don't want to go anywhere with you."

"Why not?"

"Because I—I really like Jessie." He turned and looked directly at Jessie. "I like her a lot."

For all her claims that she didn't care, Jessie looked pretty happy.

"How sweet," Becky said sarcastically. She took in Joe next to Mo. "What happened to Mr. Blond and Gorgeous? Did he dump you, or is he your city boyfriend and this here's your country boyfriend?" Becky lowered her voice. "How you could get two, I'll never know."

"I'll tell you how," Joe said matter-of-factly. "Mo is amazing."

"So you don't mind that your girlfriend was making out all week with this blond babe in Edmonton?"

Joe's neck went bright red, and the color quickly spread to his face.

"Making out?" Mo said. "Ugh, you are the worst possible roommate I could have gotten at that camp. How in the world did I get so unlucky?"

"Maybe you just don't know how to make friends." With that, Becky turned and walked off.

"I think she's right," Mo said.

"What are you talking about?" Hannah asked. "Who would want to make friends with a monster like that?"

"She's right about me not knowing how to make friends. I don't know how it happened—it wasn't anything I did—but somehow I've got the absolute best group of friends in the world. How did I get so lucky?"

"Aw, group hug," Darius said. They all shared a group hug.

Mo had her hand on Joe's back and felt the angry heat coming off him. She wondered if he was mad at Becky or mad at her.

40

Baptism Day

"There is no better day for a missionary," Elder Bennett said as if he was telling Nathan something he didn't already know. "Baptism day!" With his tie hanging loose around his neck, Elder Bennett shuffled through the mail on the table. "Hey, Matheson, you have another letter from Sarah."

Nathan fussed with his tie. For some reason, it wasn't looking right today. He misjudged the length and got the smaller back piece too long. He pulled it apart and started over.

"Here." Elder Bennett dropped the envelope on the desk next to Nathan.

Nathan glanced at the letter. Sure enough, it was Sarah's loopy script. He turned back to his tie.

"You're pretty mad at her, huh?"

"She doesn't trust me, Bennett. Trust is pretty important, don't you think?"

Elder Bennett picked up the envelope. "This letter was mailed before the other one. It came by regular mail."

"I don't want to ruin this day thinking about Sarah." Nathan took the letter from his companion. There were probably references to Carly in this letter. Sarah would write about how she and Carly went shopping or some other blatant lie. They might have gone shopping, all right, but it wasn't two girls out trying on jewelry or hair clips or whatever it was that girls did at the mall. Elder Bennett tucked the letter into Nathan's pocket and left the room.

The envelope was too big for the top suit coat pocket, so it buckled, distracting Nathan from his tie. This time the front portion of the tie was too long. "I'll trip over it," he mumbled as he roughly pulled it apart for the second time.

Not wanting a dumb letter on his mind during the baptism, he took Sarah's envelope out of his pocket and set it on his bed.

Elder Bennett returned to the room and sat on his bed across the room from Nathan.

"She's kept this big secret from me all this time," Nathan said.

"So throw the letter away and never write to her again. She'll get the picture pretty quick."

Nathan felt a stab of pain at the thought of never hearing from Sarah again, either by letter or face to face. "That's what I should do," he said. "She and I are too different. It's better to break it off now rather than wait until—"

"—you love her?"

Elder Bennett had said it as a question, but Nathan felt it as a declaration deep in his heart. "I can't fall in love with someone who keeps things like this from me."

"Do you want me to chuck that letter?"

Nathan stared at his companion's outstretched hand and then slipped his finger under the flap and ripped open the envelope. There was a short note and a newspaper clipping inside. The note said:

I saw this column in the newspaper. It sounded like something you would say about the September 11th tragedy. I hope you are completely recovered now. Miss you, as always. I'll write more later.

Love,
Sarah

Nathan stared at his own words. She had sent him the Nate Mathews column he had written about the effects of 9-11 on children. "It sounded like something you would say," Sarah had written. Maybe she knew he was Nate Mathews.

"It's my article," Nathan said.

Elder Bennett held out his hand, and Nathan passed him the article. He read aloud:

Childhood Innocence Takes a Big Blow
By Nate Mathews

One week ago the world had a shock. In the days after the attack on the United States of America, there is one question children asked that we'll never be able to answer. That question is "Why?" We may be able to say who was behind the attack and how it was orchestrated, but "why" will never be satisfactorily explained, especially to children.

Most children heard the news not from their parents, but from teachers they had known for less than a week. There they received facts and speculation but no comforting arm around their shoulders or a reassuring hand holding theirs.

When these children came home from school, they saw images on the television that looked like Hollywood special effects but were a spine-chilling reality. They saw airplanes crashing into buildings, people crying out in shock and horror. The question foremost in their minds was "Why?" And parents had to admit, "Someone did it on purpose."

A child's world should be full of beauty. He or she should experience awe at the changing of the seasons, feel happy to learn new things at school, and find joy in people he or she can trust. A child's biggest problems should be keeping track of a fancy pencil, remembering to do homework, and getting to the monkey bars at recess first. The thought that someone could plan to hurt so many innocent people is a blow to childhood innocence.

Then, children learned that terrorists were onboard those airplanes, flying them as deadly weapons to hit specific targets. How can they comprehend such a thing? Children may have seen a bully on the playground hurt someone else, but what possesses people to hurt themselves? It is irrational. They wonder what MADE them do it. Who forced them? They ask if they thought they would be able to escape. Someone taking his own life is shocking enough, but to do it in the act of killing so many others is a new horror for a child.

In the midst of the destruction of buildings and the remorse of victims, our children also saw cheering on the streets of Afghanistan. Cheering! And they want to understand why.

When my mother mentioned that the United States is the country where some of our relatives live, my young brother asked if Grandma was there. She answered, "No."

"Then why are you so sad?" asked my brother. And that was the scariest "why" of all. Have movies and television programs desensitized us to the sadness of human suffering? We should all be sad. The people we lost may not have been part of our immediate family, but they were part of the human family.

Excitement over new playground equipment should have been the feelings children experienced as they went back to school this year. Instead, they are worried about what "an act of war" really means.'

Elder Bennett shifted on his bed. "You wrote that?"

Nathan nodded.

"And her letter? Any glaring lies in there?"

"Yes," said Nathan. "Mine."

"Hmm. That's kind of ironic."

"It is. But I'm not sure it changes anything."

An hour later, Nathan was dressed in a thick white jumpsuit, listening to hymns being played softly on the piano by the bishop's wife. A few chairs away was Elder Bennett in a similar outfit, and with a smile on his face that seemed to radiate. Between them were the Ryan family; those old enough to be baptized were also in white. There was a lump in Nathan's throat.

The family's little friend, Ben, had approached him in the foyer a few minutes earlier. He was wearing a striped dress shirt and a little blue clip-on tie. "I wish I was old enough to be baptized today too," he had said. "Will you still be here when I turn eight?" Nathan ruffled his hair and then smoothed it back into the neat style he was wearing today. "I hope so," Nathan said.

Ben said. "It's going to start soon, isn't it? I better go sit with my mom."

The meeting began. There was an opening song, a prayer, a talk on baptism by Elder Pack, and then finally it was time to file out of the chapel and actually baptize these wonderful people. Nathan would baptize the father first. He and Clark Ryan entered the font, which had been filled with warm water. Nathan held his right arm in the air at the square and said the words of the baptism prayer loud enough for everyone to hear. Then he leaned Clark back into the water until he was immersed and brought him up again. He was a large man, and the water splashed up on Nathan when he stood up. The man's expression was fresh and pure. He shook Nathan's hand before he left the water.

Next, Nathan held out his hand to help Mrs. Heather Ryan down the steps into the font. As he brought her into position, there was a movement in the crowd of people watching. A familiar dark-skinned face came into view, and Nathan found himself without a voice. There was the woman he had found in the North Tower of the World Trade Center. There was no ash in the glossy black hair, no look of pain and despair on her features, but it was the same face. And holding her hand was Ben, beaming.

One of the men witnessing the baptism pointed to the card in the corner that contained the words to the prayer in case the one baptizing forgot. Nathan glanced at the words and then back at the woman. *She is here! She is Ben's mother!* "Elder?" the man said, pointing at the words.

Nathan nodded. He said the words to the prayer and baptized Heather Ryan.

When the service was over, Ben and his mother approached Nathan. She took his hand in both of hers. "I've been looking for you," she said, sitting in the seat next to Nathan in the Relief Society room where the service had been held.

"I can't believe you're here," he said, reminding himself to close his gaping mouth. That's why Ben looked familiar. He had seen a framed picture of him next to this woman when he found her.

Nathan couldn't wait to tell Sarah about this encounter. He felt no lingering anger about the Charlie/Carly issue. Nathan did forgive her, and hopefully, she would forgive him for keeping Nate Mathews a secret.

"That awful day," the woman said, "I slipped in and out of consciousness. I remembered your black tag and the words 'The Church of Jesus Christ.' I didn't see your name, or I didn't remember it, anyway. I found out that Mormon missionaries wear these kinds of tags. I started attending Church meetings in the other building, closer to our place. Ben liked to go, and I liked the feeling in the services. I gave up on ever finding you, but then Ben said there would be missionaries at the baptism and I thought I might be able to ask around and find out who you were. Now fate brought us back together again." She had tears in her eyes and she paused to regain her composure. "Thank you. They are such trite words for saving my life and saving my boy from a life of hell with his father." She covered her lips. "I guess I shouldn't say that in a church, should I?"

"My dad hits people," Ben explained, "and he's always drunk."

Nathan couldn't think of a thing to say. He was still staring at the woman he had needed to save, the woman that had been the root of his inspiration to get in shape. He never thought he would see her again. He had wondered if he had really done all he needed to do on September 11th. Maybe he could have saved more than one person.

A warm feeling spread through his body, and he knew that this woman, Ben's mother, was the sole reason for Nathan's being there. Now that he saw her with Ben clinging to her hand, words of inspiration filled his mind. *One person is generations and generations!*

The woman was speaking. "Ben has told me about the lessons you teach. I'd like to learn too. If you have time."

Nathan hadn't spoken and his mind was whirling. "You are a very special person," he said to Ben's mother. "I am humbled to be in your presence. Generations swing in the balance right now."

"What Elder Matheson means," said Elder Bennett, who was suddenly at his side, "is we'd love to meet with you. When can we come over?"

About the Author

Susan Bohnet holds an associate's degree in arts and letters with a major in psychology from Ricks College, and a bachelor of science in human resource development from Brigham Young University. She has studied creative writing at the University of Alberta. *Kaleidoscope* is the sequel to Susan's novel *Mosaic* (Walnut Springs Press, 2016). Her first novel, *My Life as a Troll*, was published in 2014 by Five Rivers Publishing. She also co-authored the novel *Lethal Influence* (Edge Science Fiction and Fantasy Publishing, 2016). In 2017, Susan published two books of family humor, *Generation Why* and *Delivery Room with a View*. She lives in Alberta, Canada, with her husband, five children, and a cute (but rather naughty) Yorkshire terrier. To learn more about Susan and read excerpts from her books, please visit susanbohnet.com.

www.ingramcontent.com/pod-product-compliance
Lightning Source LLC
Chambersburg PA
CBHW051642260626
47170CB00004B/1297